Published by Little Toller Books in 2017
Little Toller Books, Lower Dairy, Toller Fratrum, Dorset

Typeset in Garamond and Perpetua by Little Toller Books

Printed by TJ International, Padstow, Cornwall

All papers used by Little Toller Books are natural, recyclable products made from wood grown in sustainable, well-managed forests

A catalogue record for this book is available from the British Library

ISBN 978-1-908213-46-4

01

Acknowledgements

Many thanks to the Little Toller subscribers who have supported this publication: Patricia Millner, Philip Paskowitz, Rob Rowe, Robert Goddard, Nima Reid, Claire and John Plass, Harriet Owens, Neil Confrey, Tanya Bruce-Lockhart, Janice Stockford, Joe Wright, Rosemary Fern, Michael Hunt, Ian McMillan, Melly Nile and Hugo Rhys, Naomi Nile, Georgina Tuson, Bob Buhr, Christine Shaw, Alexa de Ferranti, Jonathan Clarke, Ron Riley, Keith Halfacree, Howard Wix, Mattijs Baarsma, Richard Brett, Richard Brown, Barry Taylor, Gareth Watson, Paddy Bullard, Elizabeth Shaw, Rosalina Pounder, Graham Powell, Timothy Boswell, Peter Reynolds, David Broom, Penny Hodgkinson, Suzanne Stokes, Iñigo Roque Egusquiza, Leonie Hicks and Jo Sweeting.

Havergey

JOHN BURNSIDE

A LITTLE TOLLER **MONOGRAPH**

for Carne Ross

AUTHOR'S NOTE

Though it does not feature on any maps that have yet been drawn up, Havergey is, nonetheless, as real a place as any, and a good deal more real than some.

Utopia, on the other hand, is not a place at all. It is the sum accord of a community of human creatures: what they trust, what they believe, what they see, what they know.

Needless to say, animals have no need of Utopia.

Human history becomes more and more a race between education and catastrophe.

H.G. WELLS

THE WATCHER

This morning started grey and drizzly, but now the long winter light falls across the harbour, picking out the white hull of a sailing boat on the stocks. I know that boat, of course, Annie Marchant has been labouring over it for weeks now, and she's doing a great job, though this is the first time she's ever attempted that kind of work. Which only goes to show that, when you pursue something for its own sake, you can do almost anything (with a little help from some friends). A different white, not fulmar-white, or cream, and certainly not apple blossom, but something close to Chinese white with time aged into it, like the white of snow after the first rain, when it's not yet fully melted – that's what my eye knows as the white of the lighthouse at the harbour entrance. It's never lit these days, of course; it's just there, as a presence, a piece of history. We should always remember our history; by which I mean the days before we were born. We should honour those who came before us and, in the same thought, we should remember their mistakes, so we never forget that errors are made, not by fools, but by people like us, when they forget how systems work. Ecosystems, drainage systems, warning systems, social systems – it doesn't matter. As the Scholar says, blame the individual, and the problem persists; analyse the system, and you're already one step closer to finding a solution.

On these midwinter days, the harbour – the whole island – can be preternaturally serene, and I cannot help but wonder about the effects of place and weather and light (especially light) on the formation of a people, and its sense of itself. I'm not much interested in ideas like national character, but I do believe that *place*, if it's looked at closely enough, can say a great deal about how people behave. When I lived for a time on the East Coast of Scotland, the longest I ever stayed in one place until I came here, I would walk to the harbour every day, and it fortified me, the blueish light off the water and the sense of space above that little port town. Yet it was nowhere near as wide and lit a space as this, and the water was never so still as it is this late winter afternoon. In the evenings here, the water can be periwinkle blue for an hour before it darkens, utterly smooth, though not in the hard sense, like glass, but with a perfect surface tension, a perturbability to it, like mercury. Yes: like quicksilver. At such times, it feels as if I can see for miles: all the way to the mainland, in fact, though now that there are no lights over there, *the mainland* is nothing more than haze and speculation. Still, I can see for miles and I am more than usually attentive to the subtlest shifts in the landscape, the smallest movement, the least change.

This is my talent and that makes me a Watcher. What I watch for, normally, are changes in the seasonal colours, shifts in the atmosphere, for how, sometimes, the sky offers fair warning of what it has in store for us. In winter, I look up into the great vault of the sky and pick out the stars, recalling names I learned years ago from my uncle, who was one of the first nomads to venture north after the last great plague was finally over. I love to look up and see the constellations, the planets, the occasional shooting star, partly because they remind me of him – his name was Amiel – and partly because they feel like a covenant of some kind, a promise that there's still life out there, in all that wild continuity across the water that divides us from the mainland. That evening, however, what I saw had nothing to do with that covenant, or with the weather, or the changing land. What I saw was almost nothing, in fact, just the merest hint of a blue that was not there before – and that was why I knew it was human-made. So I turned from the harbour and headed inland, to see what it was.

Every season has its given pleasures: if winter is a time for skygazing, spring is when we turn back to the earth, to bud-break and wet meadows and the wide parish of waking and arousal that surrounds us, seeds chitting in wet loam, night creatures scanning the dark for contact and nourishment, tiny ascents through leaf litter and frost and the sudden return of Platonic colour, leaf-greens and blues and golds emerging from a dank tide of mole-black soil and furze-water. Spring is renewal in any tradition. Spring is the resurrection. Autumn brings cool winds after the heat of the summer and, as soon as October arrives, the children are already looking out for the first frost, when we start preparing for the Leaf Festival, days of darker colours and shifting lights and the scent of burnt sugar everywhere, marking the year's end, the beginning of earth's long sleep, the glorious silence that falls over everything, especially in the centre of the island, in the thick woods where, now and then, walkers still chance upon the wild elk that Grandfather Follansbee introduced, a century and a half ago. According to The Archive, summers were colder then than they are now: cold and wet and unpredictable, which sounds rather dreary. Now, when the storms come, usually in late July, the skies open utterly, the entire horizon resounds with thunder and trees in the old Arboretum are occasionally ripped apart by lightning. But most of the time, the summers are hot, calm and fairly predictable. Summer is the children's season: naked boys dive from the harbour wall into the sea, whole families take picnics out to the edge of the cliffs on the north side, people fly great four-line kites and go parasurfing on Golden Beach. Still, our summers are not long, and there is much work to do, growing vegetables and fruits in the walled garden, tending the orchards, foraging for food to dry or bottle, supplies that will keep us through the cold months. To every thing here, there is a season: but summer is the busiest time, on the land, at least.

If those charts in The Archive are to be trusted, winters are harder than they used to be: cold and long and sometimes fatal to the weakest of Havergey's inhabitants, mostly animal, sometimes human. However, we make do – and for us, winter is a special time, a season of testing and training, of learning how to deal with extremes by working together. Anyone who managed to find their way to Havergey, especially during the first several years after The Dark Time, is probably some kind of maverick, self-sufficient and able to endure the solitary life, someone used to making his or her own decisions, someone who might be cautious by nature – and anyone travelling on the mainland during the years after the great plagues had good cause to be careful of others. But it takes nothing away from self-sufficiency to be able to work with like-minded souls and, as we have all learned, a community is strengthened when its people deal with hardship together. When the summer storms blow in, or when the land comes close to dying in the hardest days of January, we are reminded, once again, of how much we need one another.

Winter is also a time for specialist training, especially in martial arts. It may seem odd, in a community based on non-violence, that every citizen must learn at least one martial art. However, this was one of the first principles agreed when the first nomads used The Archive to draw up The Creation Myth (which is as much constitution as it is origin story: it was just that legalistic terms like 'constitution' didn't feel right, back then). Martial arts not only help us to maintain physical confidence, fitness and balance, they also act as a complement to other forms of meditation. Some follow the path of Tai Chi, or Kung Fu; some choose archery, or judo. None of this betokens violence, though it depends, of course, upon how violence is defined. We say that violence is by definition unnatural. It goes against the Tao. It *forces*. But the wind is not violent; it follows its way. The sea is not violent and, in spite of the immense damage they can cause, the great summer storms are not violent. Violence, we say, is an offence against the natural order: the only true perversion.

I will add, though, that we also study martial arts for defence, in case we should ever be faced with the need, not only to defend ourselves, but also, more importantly, to defend the land. We know what The Machine People did to the earth, to the birds, to the woods, to the other animals and to each other. Everyone here on Havergey has known what it is to be without a home, to be a nomad on land that, sometimes, was barely habitable and, in the worst places, overrun with free pollutants and marauders. We are here, now, because it seems a safe place, and it is more defensible than many we have passed through. Each of us sees this place as a gift, and we have a duty to defend it, no matter what comes.

And now, something has come, though it doesn't look particularly dangerous, for now, at least. In fact, it looks a little silly, lying on its side in the deep snow. A dark blue box, just large enough for a stout man to stand or lie down in, with writing on the front and odd little windows, old-fashioned panes like the Advent Calendar in the former nursery. I can just make out the writing; it says:

POLICE PUBLIC BOX
CALL

but I don't know what that means. It looks odd and I can't quite shake the idea that this is some kind of a joke, but there's no time for joking now, because, apparently, there is something, or someone inside.

PILOT'S NOTEBOOK
1st January 2017 / 1st January 2056

When I got into the capsule, I found a note pinned to the control panel but, stupidly, I didn't know who it was from until I read it. Abigail, of course. Towards the start of the project (the code name, 'primer', was suggested by Abigail herself, in fact, after her favourite time travel movie) she had adopted me, out of pity, or kindness, or maybe, child prodigy that she was, she just felt lonely, and needed someone to talk to, even if most of those conversations were a combination of self-mockery and silliness. Not that she ever seemed particularly lonely, or even unhappy, to be honest, and I never could figure out why she paid me so much attention. Maybe it was a father thing – she had been taken away from her family at an early age, to go to the genius school she had attended, and it wasn't beyond the bounds of possibility that I was some kind of parental stand-in for her. Surrogate Dad, that kind of thing. Which was odd, because I had never been a father – and by the time I got caught up in PRIMER it seemed unlikely that I ever would. But that is another story, for now at least.

Anyhow, I should have guessed right away that, if anybody was going to leave me a note, it would be Abi.

you must be the most unlikely pilot ever. good luck.
A
p.s. take your time :)

She was right, of course: I *was* the most unlikely pilot ever, but then, I wasn't going to be flying anywhere. I wasn't going to be doing very much at all, in fact, other than setting the instruments, running the countdown and – well, that was the question. And what?

That would depend on my craft. Tardis B. That's what the technicians who designed the external framework had christened it – and they had made it look like one of those old police boxes you still saw on the street when I was a child in Bromley. Some of the engineers even started calling me Doctor; though to be honest, most of the jokes were lost on me, because I hadn't really watched that show, growing up. *Doctor Who*, I mean. I hadn't watched much TV at all, in fact. My parents watched it all the time, but I preferred lying in a dark room with headphones on, listening to Amon Düül II, or Indian raga music. At one point, my mother decided I was mentally ill, but she gave up trying to have me seen to when the doctor (our GP, that is, not Patrick Troughton) told her that I wasn't insane, it was just that, because I had an IQ of 168 (I have no idea where he plucked that figure from), I was *different*. I'm not sure which of these she thought was worse.

We don't put much stock in IQ here, but I imagine 168 would be about average in this team. Oh, yes; we're smart all right. We've heard there's a group of very smart people in China who have come pretty far on a similar project, but we don't have any details, obviously. Still, as far as any of us are aware, nobody has reached the stage we are at now. By which I mean, ready to try it out and skip the next fifty years of history. Which is what I am about to do, in a matter of minutes. Oh, yes. We're smart all right.

At the time of launch, I had been working on PRIMER for six years. It was the most satisfying work I had ever done and, though I am by nature a solitary person, I found my colleagues on the project at worst, inoffensive, at best, companionable. In fact, I suppose it could be said that, at that point, the PRIMER project was the happiest time of my life. I was working towards a meaningful end: to travel in time, which had once seemed a mere pipe dream, was now, within certain strict parameters, at least feasible, and possibly even do-able. I had worked in various fields in the past, with varying degrees of success and recognition; now, for the first time in my life, I was fully engaged.

'Life, friends, is boring.' So says Henry, the protagonist of John Berryman's *Dream Songs* and it's a sentiment that I admit to having shared from time to time. Life is boring, charged with anxiety, unimaginably tedious and conducted, far too often, in an atmosphere of pointless competition. The solution? Obvious. Eat more. Drink lots. Take any and all available drugs. Sit for days at the computer playing fantasy football or war games. Why not? I remember laughing, a few years ago, when the government introduced a plan to spend four *billion* pounds of taxpayers' money to 'nudge' us back to a healthier lifestyle. It's a lot of money and, certainly, it's a lot to waste, but there was no doubting that it *would* be wasted, because, back then, in what I now know were our final months, living on the very cusp of The Collapse, we weren't just unhealthy in our bodies, we were sick overall. In our minds and our nerves and, dare I say it, in our souls. What we needed wasn't a gentle adman's nudge, but a radical cure. What we needed, in fact, was a spiritual shock of Damascene proportions.

I was as unhealthy as anyone – more so, in fact, than most. Once, I had run five miles every morning. Twice a week, I swam fifty lengths of my local pool and, whenever the opportunity arose, I'd be off walking in the hills, or the mountains, depending on where I was working. Then, seemingly in a matter of weeks, all that stopped. I'd had some upheavals in my life, what with moving to a new job and parting from someone I had *wanted* to care about (that I didn't quite succeed is still a mystery to me) but there was no good reason for what happened during those few weeks. I had never smoked, I didn't really enjoy alcohol (too hard to control) and I didn't take street drugs (ditto), but I did know a fair bit about the nice, clean, highly controllable products that anyone with access to a pharmacy could obtain. Someone like my friend Susannah, for example. And that was where I started, for no other reason than that I was overworked, constantly distracted, justifiably suspicious of authority and – bored. Suddenly, everything seemed obvious: the game was fixed, the ball belonged to someone else and the prize wasn't worth having. So – what to do? During the 'Houseboat Summit' of 1967, Timothy Leary was challenged on his famous dictum 'Turn on, tune in, drop out' and, after some discussion, he suggested a revision: 'Turn on, tune in, drop in'. That made sense to me: we had to get outside the game to see how boring it had become, but if we wanted to change things for the better, we had to drop back in and ask the question that really mattered. Which was: if you have to make an effort to stay healthy, what are you staying healthy *for*?

Not that it lasted very long. The drugs, I mean. They lifted the boredom for a while, but after that they became just another habit, a regimen that I had carefully worked out to create an artificial balance in my life. My inspiration was the pianist Glenn Gould, who kept careful notes on everything he ingested, hour by hour, constantly playing one drug off against another. Then Susannah's predations in the pharmaceuticals store came to light and though, as a mere client, I was let off with a warning, I resolved to get clean. And I did. And I was bored again – until I heard about PRIMER. Naturally, I jumped at the chance, even though it meant relocating to England, a homeland I thought I had very definitely left behind. But then, the lab was just a short drive away from Bromley and, although my parents were dead and I had never really known them anyway, I decided it would be interesting to get re-acquainted with the old neighbourhood.

But what am I thinking? And where are my manners, as my mother used to say? I really ought to have introduced myself to whoever, if anyone, reads this. My name is John –

No. Let's leave that, after all. It doesn't actually matter what my name is, does it? I am gone from that world now. I was sure, from the first, that even if it was possible to send someone (or something) forward in time, it would be impossible to convey them back without deeply upsetting the order of things. Besides, it does no harm to remind myself, before I put pen to paper (yes, as quaint as this would sound to those I left behind, I am writing these notes with a pen, on home-made paper in an ink made from oak galls by Annie, one of Havergey's many artists). As I say, before I put pen to paper, I have to remind myself that anyone who ever knew my name is now long, long dead. This is because I left everything I knew (as is now obvious, that was no great hardship) on New Year's Night, 2017, and I have to assume that there wouldn't be very much to go back to, given what I now know about The Collapse. (That term, more or less interchangeable with The Dark Time, is used here on Havergey to denote the period before the first nomads arrived on the island, which would have been around 2041, though it more strictly refers to the period from around 2024 onwards, when several waves of disease swept the globe, killing an estimated ninety percent of the population in a period of around eight to ten years.)

So I think it is safe to assume that I will not be making any effort to return, even if I believed that was possible. Now, I belong to Havergey; though I suppose I could build a boat and sail or row over to the mainland to continue my research. From here, it looks green, and unoccupied, though we are too far to be able to see for sure. But I can't help feeling that, all this time, all my life, I have been waiting to come here. That I belong here. This is a heaven created by nomads and ever since I was old enough to leave anything, I have been as nomadic as the best of them. In place, that is. Now I can add to those credentials that I am, today, a nomad in time – perhaps the first ever. Yes, it was a time machine that brought me here (how else would one find Utopia?) and it seems that it will leave me here too. Which does not surprise me because, among those who most forcefully argued that, while it was theoretically possible to go forward, to travel *back* in time was an impossibility, I was the most convincing. After all, how could we go *back*? That would disrupt the entire fabric of the universe in ways that were too ugly even to contemplate. The one hope was that an individual, such as myself, might find some way of conveying *information* back to the point of origin. Information about weather, say – which is the ostensible reason for this experiment.

It must have seemed odd, then, that while I was the most persuasive of those who argued that a PRIMER pilot would never be able to return from the future, I was also the first to volunteer. No; I was the *only* volunteer. Everyone else had wanted to go back in time, to some golden age in his or her mind's eye, some storybook realm they only knew about from – well, storybooks. Nobody wanted to go forward. Of course, I understood why they might want to travel into the past. For those of us in our middle years (which was pretty much the entire team, other than Abigail), the world had come to seem increasingly ugly. There were older people who would have argued that it was worse in the days of Auschwitz and Hiroshima, but they were few by then and, besides, our eyes were fixed on the shame – to me, the unbearable shame – of what we had done and were continuing to do to the land, to the oceans, to other species, to – well, everything. I had always been a supporter of the Gaia Hypothesis, but I hadn't seriously believed that the way the planet might find its equilibrium was by eliminating humans altogether. Now, that seemed the only possible solution: elimination, or a massive diminution. Neither were pretty to contemplate.

People paid lip service to change, naturally. But even while we recognised some of the problems, we refused even to consider the major causal factor. A few spoke up, but the fact was, overpopulation was not a sexy subject. For one, I noticed that, when I talked about it, people always assumed that I was trying to deprive someone in the third world of their God-given right to breed, while I actually would have advocated reducing population numbers among those of us who were using the largest part of the planet's resources. Let's plan to have fewer suburban gardeners spraying deadly chemicals on their driveways and lawns. Let's reduce the number of those who eat processed foods made from canola and corn oil monocultures. Let's slow down the growth of those populations where everybody has two SUVs, minimum, eight televisions scattered about the house, four or five computers – all of them *on* – and various other devices emitting heat into the atmosphere and using energy to no good end. Some days, I wanted to run into the street and scream: July 16th: 7,436,948,267 and counting. Everybody knew it was happening, and everybody was afraid to talk about it. When one commentator predicted that, if we didn't reduce our own numbers, nature *would*, using every tool it had (such as famine, disease, and wars over dwindling resources), my former partner threw the magazine she was reading across the room and refused ever to read a word that man wrote, ever again. A few others – sometimes from rather surprising walks of life – were also concerned. Mikhail Gorbachev surprised everybody when he said: 'The ecological crisis, in short, is the population crisis. Cut the population by ninety percent and there aren't enough people left to do a great deal of ecological damage.' His point made perfect sense. It was, of course, ignored.

So, yes. I volunteered. My official mission was to travel forward to the year 2050, or thereabouts, to see what had happened weather-wise by then and, if it were humanly possible, to return, or at least to convey my findings back to PRIMER, who would use the data to inform an international committee of scientists, politicians and 'other stakeholders' (i.e. Big Business) on what measures might be taken, if any, to protect what was left of what we had – or at least, of what the ninety-nine percent wished they had. To protect, in short, our cultural, social and human capital to the best of our ability under such conditions as we were about to face – something like that, anyway. Clearly, I wasn't much convinced by the committee's high-sounding language; to me, those guys were just another in a long line of politically compromised bodies that had been set up time and time again for what appeared to be the most cosmetic reasons. All I wanted was to see if PRIMER worked. I was curious. I *needed* to see what would happen, mainly because I had no other needs to speak of.

A few of the engineers would joke about what I might find. 'Maybe it will be a society run by chimpanzees in uniforms, and they'll make you a slave, and everything,' one guy said. His name, inevitably, was Mike.

'Maybe you'll find an emerging society,' Abigail said. She was sitting at her desk, right alongside mine, doodling on a sheet of graph paper. 'They have all they need to live, only problem is, there's a shortage of men. Maybe you'll finally fall in love and have loads of kids –'

'I doubt that,' Mike said. He was well-meaning enough,

but he was trying to show off to Abigail, on whom he had something of a crush. I think he resented my friendship with her, even though it was nothing more than that. A friendship. 'More likely they'll have all the kids they can handle, just not enough protein…'

Abigail ignored him. 'Maybe you'll find Utopia,' she said, all of a sudden, as if she had just thought of it. Maybe she had.

'Maybe,' I said.

She smiled, a little sadly, I thought, and it struck me that, in spite of our friendship, I didn't really know very much about her. 'Well,' she said. 'If you do, let me know. I'll be right behind you.'

The powers that be decided that the *launch* (such an exciting word) should happen somewhere fairly remote and, eventually, an estate belonging to a friend of the Home Secretary was selected as being sufficiently out of the way not to attract undue attention. I wasn't sure that Havergey was the right spot, to be honest, but it seems there was a political background to all this, as well as the practical details. The owner of Havergey estate, one Hugh Follansbee, had gone to school with the Home Sec. (actually, he owned the entire island: village, land, harbour and, presumably, the villagers too). Personally, I didn't meet, or have any dealings, with the 2017 inhabitants of Havergey (who were all at a New Year's Eve party given by this Follansbee person for his serfs and other associates in the lower hall of the great house and, I have to say, the feudal nature of Scotland was a matter of perpetual puzzlement to me). I was away out on the far side of a wide meadow, covered now with more than an inch of snow, on the site of what had been passed off to the locals as an archaeological dig. So I knew almost nothing about Hugh Follansbee that night, and nothing at all about his beautiful daughter, or the innocent people he had betrayed, or any of the other denizens of 2017 Havergey until much later, and then only through their own muddled attempts to make sense of things in a variety of badly written diaries and memoirs. Some of them would have been up at the house that very night, bringing in the New Year with all the optimism they could muster – and I hope, now, that they had a good Hogmanay, for there were dark days ahead, days of grief and loss worse than anything any of them could ever have imagined.

I was thinking all this at the moment when I finished the countdown and activated the sequence. As soon as that was accomplished, I had been hoping to make detailed observations of what it was like to travel in time – but that didn't happen. Instead, I lost consciousness almost immediately, and when I awoke, the door of Tardis B had blown open, and I was looking at a man in a red snow suit.

WELCOME TO HAVERGEY

If I were asked to make a short list of the effects of time travel on the human body, I would say: dizziness, nausea, confusion, probably a distinct rise in blood pressure (stupidly, I'd not thought to bring along the necessary instruments to measure such things) and a general heightening of the senses. For example, the red of this man's suit, which looked so out of place here, was a deep, vibrant red, the white of the snow scintillating, the colour of the sky in the middle distance a deep shade of lapis lazuli. I would have liked longer to think, but as soon as the capsule door opened (it seemed to do so of its own accord, though I do not remember it being designed that way: perhaps the engineers thought I might lose air pressure inside the unit and so risk suffocation), as soon as the door popped open and fell away to one side, the man was there, watching me. He wasn't afraid. If anything, he looked intrigued, maybe even a little excited. As if he had been waiting to see this strange sight for years.

I looked around. There was nobody else there, not for miles

it seemed; though I admit, I was having difficulty judging distances. All I could really make out was this man, waiting patiently to see what I would do next – and, again, I got the impression that he had been expecting me, or something like me. But that was absurd. How could anyone have expected me, when my presence there was, or had until that moment been, a contravention of the laws of physics?

The man watched as I struggled to get out of my absurd Tardis. He looked around thirty, though he could have been older, from the air he had of... What? Something I had seen before. An authority based on nothing external – that is, on nothing but the self. Not on power, or money, or strength of force. No. This was the self-validating authority I had seen, sometimes, in indigenous people. In hunters and tribal elders. In women who had endured long and seen their children endure. Now, whenever in time I had arrived, I felt a little dizzy and I had to concentrate to hear what he was saying. Finally, I made it out.

'Welcome to Havergey!' he says. He is smiling now. There is no sense of threat, no hostility, and no caution. He is not armed. All his power is in his voice, but this is not one of those deep, commanding, boss-man voices. It is just a man's voice, beyond dissimulation, and beyond doubt.

I cannot speak. I feel nauseous still, and a little dizzy, though that is wearing off. All I can do is nod.

The man laughs. 'You've obviously come a long way,' he says – and I can't tell if he is joking.

I nod again. Or at least I try to – all my energy, now, is directed at keeping myself upright, as I struggle out of the craft and find my feet.

'Don't worry,' he says. 'Take your time. Recover your breath.'

I lean back against the time machine and let my upper body sink. Breathe. Yes, if I could just –

'Don't think about it,' the man says, unhelpfully. 'Just breathe.' He goes on in this reassuring vein for a few moments longer, which at first is fairly irritating; but then, to my surprise, his voice softens, and whatever it is he's doing, it seems to be working. I feel better. Stronger. Maybe he's just distracting my mind so my body can get on with all the instinctive stuff it does so much better by itself, I'm not sure, but after about a minute or so, I feel fine.

'Better,' he says. This isn't a question.

I laugh, rather helplessly. I feel like a child. 'Yes,' I say. I straighten up to my full height and look him in the face.

He is still smiling. I notice that he smiles with his eyes more than his mouth. In fact, everything seems to be about his eyes. His eyes and his voice. 'Good,' he says. 'We have something of a walk ahead of us.'

'We do?'

He turns and gestures towards a low building away to what I think is our north. 'I'm afraid so,' he says. 'But, as I said, there's no hurry.'

'So – where is that?'

'Hm?'

'What is that place we're going to?' I say.

His eyes are fixed on me now, working something out, as if he were reading a sign in a foreign language. After a moment, however, he nods slightly, more or less satisfied, for now at least, and turns away in the direction of the building. 'Oh,' he says. 'Don't mind that. That's just Quarantine.'

'Ah.' Suddenly I feel suspicious. Am I being taken to some kind of prison? Or worse? Maybe the chimps in uniform aren't as unlikely as I had imagined?

The man turns back, a little theatrically, it seems to me. He appears to be having a good deal of fun with all this. 'It won't be for long,' he says. 'You'll have a chance to recover from… your journey.' He glances back at the Tardis, a puzzled expression momentarily crossing his face. 'A chance to settle,' he continues. He smiles again. 'My name is Ben,' he says. 'I am a Watcher and it is my job to help you. You will come to no harm here. Of that you have my assurance. But for now, you must come to Quarantine. You're not really dressed for the conditions, but you'll stay warm if we set a decent pace.'

And off he walks again, leaving clear, dark footprints in the snow. I follow after and I sense that he is waiting, discreetly, for me to catch up. 'So,' he says, when I do. 'Where have you come from today?'

I almost laugh at the quaintness of the expression. As if I'd just got off a 16 bus. '2017,' I say.

'Ah.' He nods. 'We read about those.'

'About?'

'Time travellers,' he says. 'Though I thought it started a little later… 2017, you say?' He gives me a look that suggests I might not be altogether sure of my facts.

'Yes.'

'It's very small,' he says. 'You must have felt a bit cramped in there.'

'It's a lot bigger inside,' I say, but of course, he doesn't get the joke. 'Besides, I wasn't in there for very long.'

'How do you know?' he says, matter-of-factly.

We both laugh, to my surprise. There is something very likeable about this man.

'So this is a – prototype, I suppose?' he says.

'I guess so.'

'An experiment, really.'

'Well,' I say, 'as far as I know, our team was the first to… What did you read?'

'Several time travellers came, just before The Collapse –'

'The Collapse?'

'When people started to get sick. Before the world went dark. Oh, of course, you don't know about it. That was later –'

'What do you mean, sick?'

'Oh, sick,' he says. 'In all kinds of different ways. Wave after wave of diseases, none of them treatable. The population was eight billion, just as the Scholar had said –'

'The Scholar?'

'Oh, you'll learn about him.' He stops walking and gives me a pained look. 'Listen,' he says. 'You're not one of those Utopia people are you?'

'What Utopia people?'

'Well, it says in the book that a few people figured out how to move forward in time, and they came to the future looking for a new world –'

'What, with chimps in uniforms?'

'Sorry?'

'Oh, nothing,' I say. I feel childish and silly. Disrespectful, too. 'No,' I say. 'I'm not one of those Utopia people.'

He nods and resumes the walk. 'I mean, it's quite understandable,' he says. 'We all want a better world. Or we think we do. But you know, Utopia is bound to be relative.

One man's heaven is another man's hell. If you're someone who comes from a brutal totalitarian regime, Utopia is a place where you get to vote. That person doesn't know that, in the representative democracy he longs for, politicians are bought by businessmen, and swayed by lobbyists so effectively that the last thing they are going to do is represent *you...*'

I nod. 'I couldn't have put it better myself,' I say. 'So what's your idea of Utopia? If such a thing were possible?'

He thinks for a moment. 'Oh, I don't know,' he says. 'I said we all want a better world, but I'm not so sure about that. I like this world well enough. And all my life, all I've wanted was to be left alone to enjoy it. Here, on Havergey, I do. That's good enough for me.' He has stopped walking again to make this little speech. 'Tell me,' he says. 'Is it true you used to sit in dark rooms watching a little box in the corner for hours on end?' He starts walking again.

I laugh. 'Some people did,' I say. 'Not everyone.'

'And everybody complained about how stupid the box was, but they kept watching it anyway.'

'Yes,' I say.

'They really did that?'

'Some did.'

We walk in silence, while he ponders this for a while.

'And they had other boxes that they stuck to their heads and talked into all the time no matter where they were?'

'Sort of.'

'And you paid people to make music even though the music wasn't very good?'

'Some of it was good.'

'I heard that all the music was the same.'

I cannot help but laugh. He's like a child, interrogating somebody who has been to the place Where the Wild Things Are. Then, after a few more minutes of walking, his manner changes completely. We are standing outside the building he'd pointed out earlier, a round wooden structure with tiny windows on the ground floor, and one huge window, with a wooden balcony, above.

'So,' he says. 'Welcome to Havergey. The agreed protocol is that you will remain here, in Quarantine, for a minimum of eight days, after which an assessment will be made about – well, what to do next.' He smiles. 'You seem apprehensive.'

'Well, I – '

'Don't worry.' He produces a bunch of keys and lets us into the building. Once inside, he fumbles with something for a moment, then the room, a kitchen, lights up. 'You won't be bored,' he says. 'We have a nice little library here, in Quarantine. A small but satisfactory gym for the practice of martial arts.' He looks me up and down. 'Do you practise a martial art of some kind?'

'Not really.'

'Not really?'

'I used to do a bit of running… It was a long time ago.'

'Well,' he says. 'As I say, I can promise you won't be bored.' He thinks for a moment. 'Though I suppose you might be – homesick?'

I look at him. 'I hadn't thought about it,' I say.

'Did you have a family, back in 2017?'

'No.'

'Ah.'

'I was married once… It didn't… No children, thank God.'

He laughs, but it is an odd laugh and he seems startled. 'Well,' he says. It seems that he had just experienced a moment of sadness, though whether for me, or for himself, or for someone else entirely, I cannot say. He sets the lantern down on a large wooden table, then he fills a kettle. I am surprised, for no good reason, by how modern the fittings are. An electric kettle, a gas hob. But no electric lights. 'You've noticed, I see, that we don't have electric lights here. Truth is, they haven't been fitted yet. To be honest, we've never used Quarantine before. You'll be our first guest. Tea?'

I nod. 'Love some,' I say.

'I hope you don't take sugar.'

I laugh. 'As it comes,' I say. I like this man. I don't know why, but I do. He seems at once childish and wise.

'Later, I'll show you where you will sleep. In the morning, you can check out the remaining facilities.' He says this like he was reading from a guide. 'For now, though, tea. No sugar.'

After we've had tea, Ben becomes oddly business-like. He probably has something to do, somewhere else to be. Or maybe, if he is the only Watcher, he is thinking he ought to get back to whatever his duties are. After all, how is he to know that I am not the first in a whole wave of time travelling invaders? He shows me the bathroom – sparsely equipped, but the towels are huge and plentiful – and how to do various things in the kitchen and about the place. He seems particularly concerned that I will not want for tea. Then he shows me my bedroom, a simple, almost monastic cell on the upper floor. I notice there are three such cells, so if there were to be a wave of invaders, I imagine they would have to improvise. Finally, he leads me into the obvious *pièce de résistance*, a large, almost empty room, that looks out over the fields by way of a massive picture window that runs all around one side of the room so that, with the moon out now and the reflections off the snow, we barely need the lantern.

'This is the practice room,' Ben says. He is obviously pleased with the place, and I wonder if he had any hand in building it. Maybe they all worked together, building communally, like the Shakers, or the Amish.

'In that corner, there is a small library, with enough reading material to last eight days, I should think. And there will be plenty of other things to do.' He gives me another of his quick up-and-down looks and smiles. 'We'll have to see if we can't get you started in some kind of practice,' he says. 'It might help you – recover from your journey.'

I laugh. 'Don't hold back,' I say. 'I'd hate for you to mince words.'

He shakes his head. 'Havergey is a wonderful place, and we have a wonderful community here. It's not like the old days, when community was just a political word. We really do have something here. Everything is shared. We don't own property individually, other than a few mementoes. What we do have is our bodies, and our ability to be well, sometimes in harsh conditions. I used to have a friend, back in my nomad days. Phil. His standard greeting was always the same: *Be Well.* It took me a long time really to understand what was contained in that simple phrase.' He grins. 'But I had better get back to what I was doing. Being a Watcher.'

'Are you expecting more guests tonight?' I say.

He smiles. 'I sincerely hope not,' he says. 'But you'll find, here, that it doesn't do you any harm to keep an eye on the weather.'

★

Strange, now, to think of that first night on Havergey. Stranger, still, to recall how happy I felt, all of a sudden, as I stood there at that picture window, gazing out into the moonlight. It was probably a side-effect of the time travel – euphoria, rather than happiness, something more to do with oxygen in the brain, or some kind of hormonal rush, than actual well-being – but I felt suddenly glad to be alive. For the first time in years, it seemed, I was properly alone and that felt like an unexpected gift. A blessing, even. Nobody here knew me. Whatever future I'd had in 2017 was now well in the past – which, from the sound of it, was just as well. Now I was here, fifty years on, in what Ben had called a real community. I'd never known that before – in fact, the word community had always left me cold. As Ben had said, it had been a political word, as in 'community values', or the community benefits tossed out like crumbs from the tables of big developers, or community service, which wasn't service at all, since it was imposed, and had nothing to do with any sense of fellowship. But that didn't mean such a thing as community could not exist. To me, it sounded utopian, a little silly, even, but that was because I couldn't envisage such a life. Was that me, or was I just a product of my time? Who could say? But then, I was out of that time now, with a fresh start ahead. All I needed was sleep. I estimated that I'd only been awake, between fifty-odd years ago and now, for around seven hours, but I was dog-tired. Maybe that's part of happiness, or euphoria, too. The ability to sleep – and it occurred to me, not altogether as a joke, that if coming to Havergey allowed me just one really good night's sleep, then it would all have been worth it.

QUARANTINE

Ben came back some hours later. I didn't know how long, because there were no clocks in Quarantine. He was carrying a large rucksack, and a pair of canvas bags, with enough food for breakfast and a generous lunch, along with various other supplies. I had been asleep for what I guessed was five or six hours, a high for me, and I'd had the most vivid dreams, oddly liquid and luminous, and brightly coloured, in contrast to the snowy landscape all around. Still, I was a little disappointed that it hadn't lasted longer. 'Did you sleep well?' he asked.

'Wonderfully,' I said. 'Though I could do with twelve more hours.'

He laughed and began unpacking his huge rucksack. He'd brought bread, jam, milk, various bottled items, some eggs. As he worked, we made small talk, as if there was an agreement between us that there would be no big questions until we both had some kind of nutrition in front of us. That done, we sat down and he looked at me questioningly. 'You will have any number of questions, I am sure,' he said. 'It's my job, as Watcher, to answer them as well as I can. All right?'

'Okay.'

'Tea?'

I nodded. He certainly liked his tea.

'All right,' he said. 'First question, if you please.'

That put me on the spot, rather, but only for a moment. When I'd woken up, in the light, I had looked out of the big window, expecting to see houses, or some kind of buildings nearby. A settlement of some kind. So – where was this community of his, I wondered. And what was it like, exactly?

'Before you left last night, you spoke about how this was a real community – and I've been thinking about that. So, tell me, what do you mean, when you talk about – community?'

He nodded. The question pleased him, clearly. It was a good starting place. 'It's true,' he said. 'This *is* a community.' He pondered for a few seconds. 'Once upon a time, when Havergey was just a story, I wouldn't have known how to say why that was. Now, for my own part at least, I do. Community is an invention – with all of the sense of the provisional and the improvisatory that word implies – and we make it for the same reasons that we make poems, or gardens, or a choreographed series of dance steps that might finally allow us to defy gravity and, having done so, having *flown*, to choose to return to the earth, gracefully, graciously, able now to accept that what holds us here does so for a reason and, in its own quiet way, is just as miraculous as flight.

'There are personal reasons too. When the dancer flies for a moment, she transcends some limit – mortality, the vain desire to become a bird forever, the simple fact of *avoirdupois*

– but she does something similar when she lands back on *terra firma* so lightly that it seems that nothing could ever really fall. To begin with, I think, I went looking for some place like Havergey because I was lonely. And when I found it, I felt even more alone – at first. I wasn't alone, of course, and I knew as much, but I felt that I was surrounded by others so unlike me in their approach to life that I might as well have been wholly isolated. *At first*. Gradually, however, I began to see that, even if they talked and acted and looked altogether different from the kind of people I thought I had been looking for (and I had imagined them keenly, sorrowfully: whole minsters and lost tribes of doomed, like-minded souls), the people I found here were my *true* brethren, partly because they *were* so different from me, and partly because, for all our differences, what we had in common was the most important thing, and that was that we were all nomads, given to veneration. Like Thoreau's saunterers, gladly wandering the face of the earth in the true nomadic spirit, seeking, not to own, but to dwell in the land justly – and, at the same time, we were, each and every one of us, as Saint Paul says of his God, "no respecter of persons".

'To begin with, I didn't see Havergey as a place, more as a group of landless people, *sans terre*, yet bound to the holy ground that Thoreau talks about, that *sainte terre* they had chanced upon – but I also notice that, where many of those who came to Havergey were once fully nomadic, avoiding any form of permanent settlement, they are now able to choose between what the Sami people call the trekways of the wind and the house by the sea – ancestral, haunted and as full of echoes as the island itself – that the poet George Seferis talks about in 'The Thrush'. That permanent nomadism was, once, not just a matter of principle, but a way of being. It would seem that I, and at least some of my brethren, have mellowed. But then, that had to do also with the island itself. You are seeing it in winter, the hardest time. And it is still beautiful now – but to be here in summer… We fell in love with this place and we felt the need to make a pledge to it, to defend it, if The Machine People ever came back to finish what they started.'

'The Machine People.'

He smiled. 'That would be people from your time.'

I couldn't help smiling too. 'Isn't that a bit much? Machine People?' I laughed.

He shook his head. 'By their fruits shall ye know them,' he said. He looked serious, but his eyes were shining. 'This island is unique. It's still alive. Everyone here has been to places that are dead, over on the mainland. And much of what isn't dead, there, is dying. But this place… As the play says, the island is full of voices. It's a large island – sometimes it's hard to remember that it's an island at all. I suppose it could be argued that any utopia would have to be an island, but this canton of the imagination is even larger, now, than it once was – larger and more populous of voices and spirits. Yet, as large as it is, every house, every *lavvu*, every yurt and cabin has a moment, mid-morning, or late in the afternoon, when a sea breeze gusts through, and a distinct ocean light plays across the wall.

'Trees, mountains, the sweet, salt sea – and, of course, rivers. We do quite well for rivers, which is fortunate, because there are no roads on Havergey beyond the harbour area. The island is criss-crossed with trails: deer lanes through tall meadows and beechwoods, desire paths and old bridleways, high mountain trails that rise into thick fog or snow and vanish, forever, it would seem, till they descend again into quite different country, but there are no roads, so all heavy or long distance travelling is done on the water. This is not as easy a system as might be envisaged elsewhere. It should be noted that, by agreement, anything that moves on Havergey does so by human effort, but that agreement is made to work by the observation of natural processes and goodwill. In fact, we might say that these are the twin guiding principles upon which Havergey's moral and practical systems are founded: a complete and unswerving trust in the natural order, and the power of the mind – sometimes, but not always, consciously directed – to accommodate and adapt to that order. All morality, all practical endeavours, all work and play are based on this principle: that *there is no human order that could be preferred to the natural order*. I cannot stress that enough. That we cannot name, or describe, or define that natural order, is accepted, but we know that we can observe it, every day, in the most mundane, as well as the most extraordinary natural events.

'But now I am straying into the realm of The Creation Myth; which is to say that, even if I am not quite getting ahead of myself, I really ought to take pains to order my thoughts, and begin at the beginning. In short, it is almost time to stop for some more tea. We stop for tea often on Havergey, mainly because we like tea, but also as a precautionary measure. The people of this island are united in their belief in the old Hagakure principle that, when action is called for, one should not prevaricate, but plunge straight in. But, at the same time, we are obliged to ask: how often is action truly *called for*? From what I have read in books, the history of humankind seems all too often to consist of actions that, though they seemed urgent to some at a particular time, were disastrous to all, and destructive of any space for informed consideration. Better to do nothing than to fiddle. The philosopher Lao Tse's term for this was *wu wei*, which has at least two interpretations. But more of this later. I want to take a moment, before tea, to mention one more governing principle of the island of Havergey, a spiritual principle, or so it might have been called once, though for us it is so much second nature that it just feels like common sense. Nevertheless, it may seem an odd idea to some outside this place, and because it is so fundamental to how we see the world, I feel it ought to be set out here, at the beginning, even before the telling of the Myth. The word we use for this principle is "interanimation". It's a term we originally found in a book by a writer from your era, but it's not a word that's been used much, which means we can add to its definition, and even redefine it a little, for our own purposes.

'In the interests of this redefinition, you have to imagine the western pastures of Havergey on a June evening, around the time of the solstice. It is a foggy evening: the cattle, cows and their calves, for the most part, loom large in the gathering whiteness and, as you walk through their midst you cannot help wondering how they see the world, and what, if anything, such mysteries as a foggy evening or the great bonfires that Havergey folk light on Midsummer Night could possibly mean to them, in their seemingly separate world, a world that, for you, seems stolid and patient and, for the most part, nearly silent. Who knows what constancy means to them? This meadow? Or those great shapes that you sense in the fog, shapes you can feel but can barely see with your limited human vision, shapes that for the cattle may be gods, or something like? This meadow, as it changes, from hour to hour, day to day, season to season? Or else, the larger gravity that bears against their flesh on evenings like this, a gravity from who knows where that, having found them out, will not budge? You try to imagine yourself as them, in some form of kinship, the days immeasurable, another kind of knowledge to set against belonging, while the body slides into the camber of its own persistency: presence as counterweight, where one or another might lift its head and see beyond the herd to something more than the ordinary dispensations. This kinship is something you can experience as a sensation – *not* an idea – but a sensory experience of a common soul, shared, but not divided, between all living things.

'This is what I mean by a new definition of interanimation: something akin to what the dictionaries tell me means "mutual animation, the idea of interanimation between body and soul" (or sometimes between texts), but, in our redefinition, encompassing everything: all species, weather, atmosphere, "rocks and stones and trees..." A new way of saying, then, that might also be a new way of thinking, for I should in all conscience repeat that, for myself, I have this experience of interanimation as a sensory event and not as an idea. So, for the sake of argument, and in hopes of ruling out the temptation of easy mysticism, I am talking about an experience in which I feel that everything is not so much connected as continuous, by which I mean continuous as *play* is, when it is at its best.

'So, given this experience, what should I trust? The sense

of interanimation, of being continuous with all other life, and even matter itself, or the times when we take this world for granted, a condition in which every single thing is restricted once more to its field of being, single and specifically apart, isolated in the fog that has now moved inward across the pastures of west Havergey and into the village itself, singling out each chimney and window and orchard tree and wrapping it in its own cloud of whiteness? That sense of disconnect seems to have been the norm for many in earlier times, when the agreed world was a celestial machine, inhabited by diagrams of fish and giant redwoods and the various classes of mammal – and human beings (diagrams from respected textbooks themselves) were to be seen, in public at least, as unswerving, no-nonsense, hard-line rationalists, no matter how blind or careless that self-limiting, reductive logic made them. Was it this hard line in rationality that caused their fall? I don't know – and it's time for tea. But there will be time for such speculations later.' He smiled. 'I have talked too much and there is much to take in. And this is only theory, where what matters is practise. I have to be somewhere this afternoon, so you can have some peace and quiet. Time to meditate, perhaps?' He looked at me pointedly.

I shrugged. 'I'm not in the habit – '

'That's fine,' he said. 'It's easy to get started. All you have to do is breathe.' He settled into his chair and breathed in. There was no great effort involved, no sense of some kind of – discipline, I suppose. Then he breathed out. 'That's all there is to it,' he said. 'If you like, you can mark the breaths, just say something silently, in your head – one for an in-breath, say, two for the out-breath. Whatever. What matters is that you pay attention to the breath without *paying attention* to the breath, if you see what I mean.' He thought for a moment. 'I always find it hard to explain. Angharad is better at it than I am. All I can say is, don't force it. Don't try to clear your mind. Don't try to have good thoughts. Just let everything happen, and let it go by. All that matters is that you breathe. In, out. In, out. That's where you start.'

I nodded.

He smiled. 'Good,' he said. 'Also, there are some books on the shelf that will tell you more about the island's history. About the people who came before. The Scholar, John the Gardener, the others. They were the ones who dreamed Havergey into being. We just came along and made that dream a reality for a while.'

THE SCHOLAR'S BOOK

After Ben left me for his other duties, I went to the library and unpacked what he had called The Archive. I was intrigued by what he had said about the people who had come before, the ones who had dreamed Havergey into being. What did he mean by that? He didn't know these people, nobody here did, but I couldn't help noting the irony that, just yesterday (or yesterday for me, at least), they had been gathered at the big house to see in a new year. Hogmanay, they would have called it, a word with no obvious meaning, unless you trace the etymology back through an old dialect of Northern France and find *hoguinané*, which in turn is derived from Old French *aguillanneuf*, which, (they say) means a gift for the New Year (*l'an neuf*). Others think the word comes from the old Flemish word for the same festival *hoogmindag*, which, if you break it down, means high (*hoog*) love (*min*) day (*dag*). That would explain the tradition of first-footing, when any tall dark stranger can turn up on a Scottish doorstep and be welcomed with whisky and cake (and he brings his own gifts too: coal, salt and bread, as token of warmth and nourishment for the coming year). I wonder if anybody at that Hogmanay party had given any thought to that tradition. Or had they just turned up in their kilts and dress shirts and eaten canapés for as long as they could stand it? From what I had heard about Hugh Follansbee, I can't imagine it was a joyful, love-filled occasion.

The Archive contained a pile of A4 notebooks, all very similar in appearance, though written in different hands, three file boxes of loose papers, several batches of photographs and various papers in faded manila envelopes, and a small portfolio of sketches and watercolour paintings of garden and street scenes. Each item had its own distinct identifying number and each was labelled with a brief description, for example, item S03 was labelled *The Scholar's Commonplace Book, c.2025*, while item P01, one of the manila envelopes, was marked *Photographs taken in Rome* (*May 2014?*). So far, so much family memorabilia, or so I supposed. But it was one of the file boxes that drew my attention. Here, the label was written boldly in what I took to be black Sharpie: it had no identifying number; all it said was PLANS FOR THE REVOLUTION, *LA FIN DU MONDE, EN AVANÇANT* in neat, if rather boxy block capitals. I opened it.

First item, a poster, quite well designed, with images of natural growth (acanthus stems and vines, it seemed like the marginal decorations in early illuminated books) proliferating elegantly up and down the left and right margins, the central area taken up entirely with the words, printed in Calibri block capitals:

IT IS ONLY WHEN WE HAVE RENOUNCED OUR
PREOCCUPATION WITH "I," "ME," "MINE," THAT WE
CAN TRULY POSSESS THE WORLD IN WHICH WE LIVE.
EVERYTHING, PROVIDED THAT WE REGARD NOTHING AS
PROPERTY. AND NOT ONLY IS EVERYTHING OURS; IT IS ALSO
EVERYBODY ELSE'S.

The quotation – if there was one – was unattributed, but it had a ring to it. The next item, however, was hopelessly amateurish: it seemed to be an outline of a short film, a script, or treatment, for a propaganda piece. In the header area someone had written, in bold dark letters: BROTHER FELIX'S RALLYING CRY. What followed was a typed script, over which various people had scribbled their comments and questions:

FELIX JEDERMANN / TIZIANA VOLPATO / FILIPPO TURATI
A Non-Political Broadcast

[Q. Do we need a title for this? Working title? – T.]
MUSIC *[Any suggestions? I'd quite like to use that great piano trio we heard in Hamburg. – F]*
[What – do you mean Tingvall Trio? Fine by me. Do we have to pay for that? – Felix.]

AN OPEN FIELD, OR MEADOW, SURROUNDED BY HEDGEROWS. SOME PEOPLE ARE PREPARING A PICNIC, SETTING OUT BOWLS AND PLATES ETC. ZOOM IN, AS YOUNG WOMAN COMES INTO SHOT, CARRYING A PAIL.

YOUNG WOMAN: I found some berries –

NOW, IN CHOREOGRAPHED, QUICK MOVING SEQUENCE:

A YOUNG MAN: I found some apples –

A SLIGHTLY OLDER WOMAN: I met a fisherman by the river and exchanged two of the bread loaves I made for some fish –

LITTLE GIRL: Tomas and I helped a lady move her cows and she gave us some milk –

ARTIST: And I sold a painting at the tourist market, so I bought some fruit juice and things to make salad –

ELDERLY WOMAN: And I baked a cake. So now we have everything we need for our picnic. And we got it all by working together, and foraging, trusting to the land and to the goodwill of others. . .

ELDERLY WOMAN TURNS, SPEAKS DIRECT TO CAMERA AS THE OTHERS CONTINUE WORKING ON THE PICNIC

. . . It's not always easy, in the world we have inherited, but it *is* possible to work together, to live a good life in harmony with the earth and with those we share it with. All we need to do is *forget* party politics, *forget* the consumerist trap that has you working for things you don't need, *forget* career politicians who want us to be at each other's throats all the time so they can exploit those divisions and keep their corporate donors happy.

ARTIST: The big question is - what kind of system do we want? Do we want to be governed by others, by men and women who are in hock to business and lobbyists? Or do we want to govern ourselves?

YOUNG MAN: Edward Abbey said: *Anarchism is not a romantic fable but the hardheaded realization, based on five thousand years of experience, that we cannot entrust the management of our lives to kings, priests, politicians, generals, and county commissioners.*

ELDERLY WOMAN: Ursula K. Le Guin says: *Nothing is yours. It is to use. It is to share. If you will not share it, you cannot use it.*

ARTIST: We are anarchists. We don't throw bombs at people, we don't advocate violence, and we don't want to live in chaos; on the contrary, our deepest and most lasting belief is in *order* – the order we find everywhere in the natural world, the order in which everything is able to be, according to its own nature.

BRING CAMERA BACK HERE, TO SHOW WHOLE GROUP AGAIN [?]

ALL: We don't want you to vote for us. We are not a party. We just ask that you stop voting for parties and so-called representatives who have consistently failed you for decades. We ask that you stop listening to the lies and let their record speak for itself. We ask that you think of the poisoned and dangerous world you live in, and wonder how it got that way. We ask that you just –

LITTLE GIRL: **Stop**! [SHE SMILES] Stop being governed. [MUSIC STOPS] Think for yourself.

Needs work. Is the music playing all the way through? – F. Agree – needs something. But it could work. Could we do the whole thing with just children? – T.

I found that funny. It seemed so naïve, so trusting. But then, how else would an anarchist talk. From what I knew about anarchism, it was all about trust. If you had no power structures, you had to have trust. Which meant, of course, that these people were being totally unrealistic.

I put aside the script and opened a book labelled, *The Scholar's Book*, more or less in the middle. The handwriting here was energetic and bold, even though the script was somewhat faded. At first, I thought it was a diary, of sorts, but it soon became clear that it was a mix of different things: diary entries, commonplaces, drafts for letters, observations, fantasies, and material that, at times, resembled the contents of one of those old dream books that people used to keep. I opened the book at random.

Chennai, January 22nd 2020

Always, in the early morning, birds in the strips of garden behind my hotel, a light in a single window at the end of the street where someone is reading a book, the windows clouded with condensation, there is the gravitas of place in itself. Place intersected with time is what we mean by Being, and it includes these bodies as such – me at my window, the other reader in his – as well as all the bodies we dream every night, as improbable as they seem in daylight.

This may be the last time I see Paola. We always say that, but this time I think it is true. As soon as Hugh discovered what was going on, we knew it would have to end – and my dear brother-in-law had posted an ultimatum: give her up now, or he tells Fabrizio the whole story – and I can scarcely begin to imagine what happens then. Paola just shrugs it off and laughs, as she does with everything, but I know she understands the seriousness of the situation. Fabrizio's standing with anyone who matters is now so high, he could do anything he liked and get away with it. He and Brother Hugh have forged a dangerous alliance. Nobody is safe.

If it must end, I suppose it is appropriate, at least, that it ends in India. So, tomorrow, we go north for ten days – and then we part. She to Rome and I – to Havergey, where I am of a mind to settle into a solitary existence, assume my scholar grey garments and bury my head in my books. Brother Hugh is rarely there now. London has need of him, or so he thinks.

If he stays away enough of the time, Havergey would suit me very nicely. Still, it's early days yet. And there's no proof at all that I could adjust to such a life. None whatsoever.

> Anarchists know that a long period of education must precede any great fundamental change in society, hence they do not believe in vote begging, nor political campaigns, but rather in the development of self-thinking individuals. We look away from government for relief, because we know that force (legalized) invades the personal liberty of man, seizes upon the natural elements and intervenes between man and natural laws; from this exercise of force through governments flows nearly all the misery, poverty, crime and confusion existing in society.
>
> LUCY PARSONS

No plan for a better world can be successful unless we remember the world that had to be replaced. Not just the grosser inequalities and political scandal, but the way such things affected our day-to-day lives. The *fine grain* of injustice. The pettiness, the dishonour, the ignoble behaviour. We do not live, much of the time, at the socio-political level. We live at the quotidian level, and it is there that we must look for symptoms of a bad system. It is in the way that a family has dinner together (or does not, but watches television, eating off trays in silence), the way a wife talks to her husband, the odd ailments we contract for apparently no good reason, and even the way two men regard one another, should they find themselves alone in a country railway station – and for that matter, whether there are any country railways stations left to wait in – *these* are the indicators of a society's health, not GDP, or any other statistics-based chimera. That is why we must continue to read writers like Lucy Parsons: she reminds us of the fine grain of what happens when the corrupt system intervenes 'between man and natural laws.'

Or, as Tsunetomo Yamamoto says: *in the end, the details of a matter are important. The right and wrong of one's way of doing things are found in trivial matters.*

February 10th

Tonight, as I was driving home from the airport, a new fall of snow began just as I came – far too early – to the ferry. So, with nothing else to do, I stopped to watch it settle on the alder trees and the snowberry bushes around the terminal building. There was plenty of time and I made the best of it, or tried to at least, gathering energy from the snow to steel me, not so much for the crossing to Havergey as for the reception I would receive there. Of course, I could now tell Yvonne that, yes, Paola and I have agreed to part, once and for all – as we did when we said goodbye at New Delhi. Nevertheless, I wasn't looking forward to going through the same old conversations again, all the reassurances, all the half-truths and lies. I feel sure, now, that Fabrizio would quite happily have Paola killed to save face, and that thought frightens me, so I tried hard to shut them all out of my mind – Hugh, Fabrizio, Cousin Felix (that loveable, treacherous devil), even my dear sister – while I entered fully into that passing moment's grace, standing by the terminal, alone for now, my headlights (I had left them on, for some reason) reaching out into the trees to where something in the darkness was gazing back at them, or rather, at me, not something I could see, but something sensed. I knew it wasn't 'just' an animal, I knew it wasn't an isolated presence at all, in fact, but a mass event, many eyes or some larger mind returning my gaze as I peered into the darkness, waiting for me to see it, finally, as it was. And still, now, as it is.

[Undated]

My principal memory of school is of how diligently they taught us to ignore the beautiful in its wilder and more immediate forms. The picturesque, the pleasing, the quietly anthropomorphic: only these were to be cultivated. But the wild, the sublime, the fathomless? Nobody railed against them, they simply weren't considered worthy of attention.

How odd, then, that those clever little blindings of our school-day afternoons would forever afterwards be considered a mercy. But that was what they were, and for most people of my time and class, that is what they remained. No victory was more satisfying for our elders and betters. Without beauty (or rather, without the sublime) all that remained was work, money, identification with the sources of power. That, more than anything, was what 'patriarchy' meant to us.

Some minor achievements were possible, however. For example, I avoided at least part of the good education they had in mind for me by utterly rejecting Newton. I did so on a blanket and, so, quite childish level, but it made little difference. My teachers, never doubting that *that* 'Magister' was right on all counts, didn't even notice my dissent.

We needed a time of unlearning; we got a time of forgetting. Now, having forgotten so much, we have to go back and reiterate the obvious.

Havergey, March 12th

Trasumanar significar per verba
non si poria; però l'essemplo basti
a cui esperïenza grazia serba

When we were in New Delhi, I asked Paola if she could translate these lines and retain the essence of what Dante is saying. She laughed. 'In English?' she said. 'No chance.'

But I thought it could be done, if not in translation, then in paraphrase, by reference to the opening chapter of *Tao Te Ching*, where Lao Tse tells us that Tao (what cannot be explained in words – *significar per verba non si poria*) can nevertheless be observed, in its natural workings, by those who are not caught up in attachment, in the desire to have the world be as you want it to be, as opposed to how it is – which is close to saying, those who are in a state of grace.

Goethe is, at the very least, on similar ground when he says: 'As soon as we consider a phenomenon in itself and in relation to others, neither desiring nor disliking it, we will in quiet attentiveness be able to form a clear concept of it, its parts, and its relations. The more we expand our considerations and the more we relate phenomena to one another, the more we exercise the gift of observation that lies within us. If we know how to relate this knowledge to ourselves in our actions, we earn the right to be called intelligent.'

What matters here, again, is that caution to the feckless spirit, that 'neither desiring nor disliking' – and there is a clear challenge here, a challenge to the scientist, who is human and attached, not to desire or dislike (in other words, not to form an idea of an acceptable outcome). The only way to accept that challenge is to attain a state of grace, before, during and after the experiment, in order fully to exercise the 'gift of observation that lies within us', that is, an observation that is not clouded by attachment. With attachment, or desire, we observe only 'manifestations', or appearances; whereas, free of attachment, it is possible to observe the essence of what is happening (I have to think of all of this in terms of verbs, not nouns, in terms of processes that are happening all at once but in hugely differing time frames, rather than as 'objects', as such; a way of perceiving that seems to me entirely in keeping with the notion *natura naturans*. 'Nature in the active sense,' says Coleridge – as if, outside our minds, there could be anything else.)

Now, add a dash of Spinoza to the mix, (Paola thinks I can't get through a single day without adding a dash of Spinoza to the mix, whatever the mix might be) – thus:

> My argument is this. Nothing comes to pass in nature, which can be set down to a flaw therein; for nature is always the same, and everywhere one and the same in her efficacy and power of action; that is, nature's laws and ordinances, whereby all things come to pass and change from one form to another, are everywhere and always the same; so that there should be one and the same method of understanding the nature of all things whatsoever, namely, through nature's universal laws and rules,

and we have the entire basis for our science, such as it need be, on Havergey, a set of principles that could be summarised in the following rough precepts:

We cannot name, describe or define the transcendent (what the Chinese sage, quite aware that he was using a nonsense word, called Tao), but we can observe its workings as it unfolds in the natural world, as long as:

We prepare ourselves, in our observations of nature, by first achieving a state of grace, a freedom from attachment, from desiring or disliking, before making any such observations.

We understand that the natural order, Tao, is everywhere the same, and finally, we accept that any human-made order, no matter how sophisticated, is at best an approximation of Tao, and at worst, a substitute, or even an offence against the natural order (all too common in the last century or so). Given the means, we seem capable of all manner of absurd destruction and degradation of 'the environment', a term I have always disliked in itself, as it defines the world only *in relation to humans*, as if all of nature were just *chez nous*.

So to summarise (though not, as Paola says, to be brief) I would say that if I were laying the basis for some future utopian community on Havergey (a community free of Hugh and his friends, a community strong enough to tolerate Cousin Felix's ravening hunger for – whatever it is he is hungry for…) If, as I say, I was trying to set Utopia in motion, I would say that this would have to be the basic principle of that community: that Nature, meaning Tao, or the overarching order of *natura naturans* that can only be observed in a state of grace, would always take priority, in our hearts and minds, over any human scheme – however worthy (or profitable) it might seem – that was not totally in keeping with that natural order. Which means we really do have to get rid of Brother Hugh, doesn't it? The trouble is, how?

[THREE PAGES TORN OUT HERE]

[Undated]

I am homesick for all the places where I might have settled, had things been otherwise. A tiny apartment on the rue Dante, that *rørbu* in western Norway, where I watched sea eagles fishing one bright summer's morning on a day when it seemed, finally, that time would stop being linear and become infinitely more interesting. That was the first summer with Paola. Now we have parted. And Yvonne? Has she parted from Felix or is she just saying what I want to hear?

But is it really the case that non-linear time would always be preferable? Is linear time really so awful? Or is my aversion to the linear merely a symptom of an adulterer's distaste, if not actual fear, of narrative? In narrative, we get found out, eventually. Things come to light. For one golden afternoon, things can be perfect. Give it a month, though…

And, had I settled in any of those places, would my life then have been confined to one golden afternoon?

*

I closed the book with a snap. My eyes were tired, suddenly – and my head was going round, trying to get a picture of who all these people were, and what relations they stood in, each with the others. Yvonne was sister to Max, the Scholar, and cousin to Felix, that was clear – and she was married to the owner of Havergey Island, the man Max calls, with obvious disdain, Brother Hugh. However, she also seemed to be having an affair with Felix – was that incestuous? I didn't even know. Meanwhile, there was a woman named Paola, with whom Max is in love, but they have parted because of a man named Fabrizio, presumably Paola's husband. Who Tiziana and Filippo were, other than friends of Cousin Felix, and self-styled anarchists, I had no idea. Perhaps that was all they were: friends. I seem to remember thinking, then, that I would have to read more, but if I did, it was the last thought that passed through my mind as, with the Scholar's book sliding off my lap and on to the floor, I fell once more into a deep, wintry sleep.

QUARANTINE

The next morning, I woke with a fever. I didn't want to stay in bed, though, in case Ben decided to leave me to sleep – I wasn't lonely exactly, but I needed the contact, a few sentences, if nothing more, of conversation, one of his odd, self-deprecating smiles. That seemed odd to me in itself, as I'd always been a fairly solitary person, happy with my own company. I also needed breakfast and tea. I was feverish, but I was still hungry and it seemed like a long time passed before Ben arrived, just as the light broke through across the snowy meadow. I had no idea what time that was, and when I asked him, he simply shook his head. 'It's morning,' he said. 'Time for breakfast.'

'And tea,' I said and then I laughed, to show I was joking. I really was quite feverish.

'Are you all right?' Ben asked. 'You seem a bit – flushed.'

'I'm fine,' I said. 'I sat up reading too late.'

He came closer and peered into my face. 'No,' he said. 'You have a fever. I hope you haven't caught a cold – '

I had a sudden rush of fear that, if he thought I was ill, I might be confined to Quarantine for longer than the prescribed eight days. A fortnight. A month... 'I do feel a little warm, now you mention it,' I said. 'But that's probably from... I imagine time travel will do that to someone.'

He smiled. 'I imagine,' he said. 'Just stay warm, and drink lots of fluids.'

He turned back to what he had been doing. Today's breakfast was almost identical to yesterday's, but with the addition of a pot of honey and a tiny square of butter.

'Are you busy today?' I asked, as he worked on the food.

'No,' he said. 'I have some time off. Angharad, one of the other Watchers, is on duty for the next two days.'

I felt relieved, even slightly elated. I had questions I wanted to ask. Questions about Hugh Follansbee, and the anarchists, and the Scholar, but I thought it best to wait till we were eating before starting that conversation.

'I thought I could tell you about The Creation Myth today,' he said, over his shoulder. 'It's the basis of everything we do here –'

'That would be great,' I said. 'Actually, I've been reading the stuff in the library. The Archive.'

'Good.'

'And I was a little confused,' I said. 'I mean... I'm still trying to sort things out in my head –'

He nodded. 'Yes, there are a lot of ideas to take in –'

'No. I mean...'

He turned to look at me. 'Breakfast is served,' he said.

I went and sat down at the place he had set for me. There were bread rolls, a little butter – the piece was tiny, which suggested that butter might be in short supply – various jams, honey, some kind of homemade cake. But then, of course, everything here would be homemade. 'I can't quite get the people clear in my mind,' I said. 'I mean, I know Yvonne was Hugh's wife, and Max – he's her brother…'

He sat down. I could see he was thinking about something. Trying to figure out, not what to say, but how best to say what he had to say next. He poured us both some tea. It was strong and very dark, like tar. 'Those people are part of the story, but The Creation Myth, the point at which the new Havergey came into being, begins after most of them are already dead. Only John the Gardener is left: Hugh Follansbee has disappeared, Yvonne and her daughter are dead, Max is still alive, but he goes travelling to India, looking for something, or someone, he thinks he has lost, and John's father, old John Graham, is retired. Now John the Gardener has taken charge of Havergey's gardens and now, finally, he is in a position to realise his dream and let nature take its course. This is where the new Havergey begins – when the old Havergey is restored.

'John records in his diary that, when Hugh Follansbee disappeared –'

'He disappeared?'

Ben nodded. 'Just like that. Very convenient, people said. It was just before the plague came to Havergey… Still it was a happy moment. John writes in his book that he has been freed from a kind of everyday prison, a place that, for each of us, is the whole world: for a schoolchild, the playground, for the vicar, his congregation, for the garden worker, or the house maid, that circle of friends and judges, equals and superiors, that govern everything in life, from when you woke in the morning to when you lay down to sleep. Then, all of a sudden, that's all taken away, or enough of it is to make what's left irrelevant, and the moment you see this, the moment you step away from all that interference, it recedes to a faint murmur in the middle distance, an odd snatch of conversation from a garden party three or four houses away, with words you can't quite make out but, from the tone, you can guess what they are, and you move on to something else because whatever is happening over there doesn't really matter any more.

'In my various wanderings, I have come to believe that, in order to become its true self, the heart must shape itself around some grain of impossible love, or pain, or refusal, as a pearl shapes itself around a piece of sand or grit, and begins its search for a perfected expression of that tiny, almost invisible object. If this does not happen, then the heart is a complex of muscles and chambers, no more. That process began for John the Gardener when he lost Chloë, I imagine.'

'Chloë?'

'You have to read John's book,' Ben said. 'He loved Chloë, but it wasn't to be. She was Hugh Follansbee's only heir, and he… Well, John was just the gardener.' He smiled ruefully. 'Yes,' he said. 'First, he lost Chloë, and then, later, he lost everything. Everyone he had ever known. He seems to have been the self-appointed gravedigger, when the plague came to Havergey, and his back must have ached, from playing Yorick to so many of his former friends and acquaintances, people he had once joked with, people he had once despised, or pitied, people he barely knew, though he'd seen them almost every day for decades. It must have weakened him, body and soul, to have to bury so many, but in his notebook he does not complain, simply marking off the names of those he had interred, week after week through that long summer and carrying on with his work in the garden. New work, now that Hugh Follansbee was gone. New, joyful tasks. But hard, too. After decades of regimentation, it can be hard, letting nature take its course.

'He records the process with real pleasure, though – to begin with at least. All the changes in the garden: changes he himself gladly allows to happen. With Hugh gone, he can do anything he likes – and I love to think of him, putting away the various mowers, letting the grass grow. He left the big roller out on the Great Lawn and sprinkled wildflower seeds around it, so it might rust there, pinned down by vetches and bindweed and convolvulus. God knows what he did with the edging shears, but over that first glorious summer, the grass grew high and, through it, the first wildflowers grew. Then as time passed, this meadow flora grew richer and more various, and John reminds himself, with childish pleasure, that some seeds can remain dormant in the soil for decades, only to flare into life as soon as conditions are right. Or rather, as soon as conditions are no longer hostile. By now, there is more to the former lawns than this meadow effect: now, John is seeing wildflowers he had never seen before in the grounds of Havergey, because the only places where a touch of wildness was tolerated were a few patches of woodland shade along the fence lines, where meadow flowers would not have prospered. With the new flora come new neighbours. Birds and animals that once kept to the safety of the outer estate now ventured increasingly into the gardens, as if, by allowing the former lawns to recover their native condition,

Havergey House had proclaimed a new, more democratic order among all creatures. Hares, especially, revelled in the new cover, and in their freedom to wander, but there was an increase in numbers and variety across the board, from frogs to bats to filmy ferns to foxes.

'Then, though it felt less deliberate – an accident of supply and demand more than anything – the next pleasure came from allowing the gravel paths to run wild, those paths that had always been so free of weeds, the gravel saturated every few weeks in herbicide. Soon they were colonised by willow-herb and thistles, various grasses, medicago, vetch and, right from the start, surprising, bright splashes of Lady's Mantle, apple green in new leaf like the green of the old Windsor inks he had used in school. The rate, and the variety, of this colonisation really was surprising.

'When the first nomads came, they found The Archive – the letters, the drawings, the notebooks – and they consumed it all greedily, because it was a history of this place, when they put it all together, but it was also full of ideas, challenges to how they intended to live in this place. That was what interested them – and it's what interests us still. We're not so concerned about the personal stories, we've all lost friends and loved ones to chance and treachery, we've all witnessed terrible moments of cruelty, but we've had to tell ourselves that it doesn't matter, now, that nothing anyone could do would bring anybody back. But the ideas – all those ideas, the commonplaces, the principles, all brought together and copied into a few notebooks, that was exciting. Maybe – maybe *home* was possible. Maybe there could be community here. The first ones to arrive had sailed, rowed, rafted, a few had even swum here – swum to a place that is famous for its dangerous currents, its cold, treacherous waters, its storms – all to get away from the mainland. But when they came ashore…'

He stopped talking and looked at the table in surprise, or so it seemed. Then he took one of the rolls – they were crispy, golden – and spread it with the thinnest sliver of butter, before adding a generous helping of honey.

'One of the older men – his name is Gregory, you'll meet him when you go through – he told me how it felt, to come to shore his first day. It was summer, and he had come by himself in a whitewater rafting canoe he'd found at an abandoned sports facility on the far side. He said he'd never seen anything so beautiful as this island – but as soon as he pulled the canoe ashore, he stood up tall as he could and looked around to see if anybody had followed. Then he scanned the shore and, after a while, he saw that there were others here, people like himself, or not like himself, because in fact they were all very different, but they all had one thing in common. They had left the old world behind. The dead, the lost, the betrayed, the traitors who, at times, really had no choice – except, of course, that there is always a choice. It might be high in cost, but – well, Gregory is old-school, you might say. He believes that each person has his or her honour first and foremost. You do what you can to survive, you do what you can to help your family, but not if it means dishonour. He told me he remembered, when he was a teenager, he heard a news broadcast from the House of Commons. He didn't really understand it all, it just seemed crazy to him that supposedly intelligent people were even discussing it, but what he does remember is that, during a debate on nuclear weapons, somebody – a Scottish MP, whose name he couldn't recall – asked the Conservative Prime Minister, whose name he didn't want to recall, if she was 'personally prepared to authorise a nuclear strike that can kill a hundred thousand innocent men, women and children' and this woman hadn't even hesitated. She had just come back with a firm and decisive "Yes!" – then the debate had continued, as if they were discussing the shoe manufacturing industry or new incentives to help turn talented young cricketers into top-notch international competitors. But not only did those people happily discuss this scenario, those same people voted by a majority of over 350 to continue building such weapons – and at that moment he remembered reading the testimony of a young girl from Hiroshima named Michiko, who talked of "people whose eyeballs had popped out their sockets. There were those who held their babies – burnt black. They themselves had no skin. There were those whose intestines had come out of their bodies, and confused they struggled to put them back in…" As I say, Gregory was just a teenager, but he liked to read and he paid attention to what was happening in the world – and he remembered then what Howard Zinn had said, how there was "no flag large enough to cover the shame of killing innocent people." At that point, he had resolved that, whatever he did, he would not contribute in any way to such a society – to such a corrupt system – in which the dishonour of mass murder was seen as a trivial matter.

'Now, that was all gone – and for a moment, as the others on Havergey came out of their huts and *lavvus* to meet him, he saw that they, all of them, working together, had a chance to do something he'd never dared hope for till then. He had seen the destruction on the mainland. He knew that, other than a handful of the lucky and the careful, the people who had run that old world were gone. Now they could start again.'

He finished his tea and poured himself some more. He looked at me and I nodded. 'How was he to know it wouldn't all happen again, same as last time?' I said.

'He didn't,' Ben said. 'But when they found The Archive, he thought they had found a possible starting point. An idea of origin. A creation myth.'

That was the end of our discussion – for a while at least. We would come back to The Archive later, but for now, I understood what he was saying. As far as he was concerned, the individual stories didn't matter, it was the ideas that mattered. The principles that 'the Scholar' had culled from his wide reading and his travels. Those principles would form the basis of a new society on Havergey – a society these people would defend with their lives, not because of some territorial impulse, but because of a simple land ethic. They had seen what we Machine People had done to the land, and they would not let it happen again – not here. They would die to defend that soil, those woods and meadows – but they would not kill innocent people for any reason. I had not met a single Havergeyan (was that a word?) other than Ben, but I could see them, in my mind's eye, women like Angharad, the Watcher, and men like Gregory, for whom nothing mattered more than a concept so old-fashioned and impractical in the world that I had left just two days earlier that it was something of an embarrassment – or a joke. *Honour.* For a moment, I felt sad that I had lived in that world so obediently, numbing myself with pills, diverting my mind with highly technical puzzles, mostly for the distraction of it all. But that feeling only lasted a moment, before I remembered what Ben had said: that those old days were over now. Like the others, I had been given a chance to start again – and that word, 'honour', so grand, so silly, so outmoded, was the key. I broke off a piece of breakfast cake and put it in my mouth. It tasted of apples and honey and something else that I couldn't identify. Ben looked at me and smiled. 'Good cake,' he said. Like everything he said, it was not a question – and, suddenly, I knew why.

*

Ben stayed till late in the afternoon, and we talked, in a more or less desultory way, about Havergey and its inhabitants, the principles, the idea of a Creation Myth. He told me stories about how some of the first nomads had come to the island – there had been many losses on the way, but there had also been minor miracles in which the seemingly impossible had happened.

'One day,' he said, 'one of the fishing boats was out, in totally calm water, the sun so hot that a haze of steam rose off the deck, making it all seem just one great apparition. On any other day, that boat would have sailed right past the raft that was sitting, utterly becalmed, utterly still, in the middle of the sound, but that day was special.' He gave a little nod, as if expressing thanks to some unseen, unnameable power, some variety of providence that, from time to time, offered a tiny miracle as respite in the midst of chaos and destruction and I was reminded of Mrs Wickham, in *Dombey and Son*, when she says: 'Hope is an excellent thing for such as has the spirits to bear it! My own spirits is not equal to it, but I don't owe it any grudge. I envys them that is so blest!'

'Luckily, those fishermen didn't sail past it, they saw it as they approached, well in time to avoid striking it, and when they came alongside, they saw something that was impossible – impossible anywhere, I imagine, but especially so in these waters. Maybe the men on board that boat – it was the *Chloë*, I recall – thought they were hallucinating, but there, in the middle of the raft sat a child, a toddler of around eighteen months, or maybe two years old. Alone. In the middle of the open sea. There was evidence that others had been on that raft at one time or another – a woman's blouse, stained with what looked like oil, a bag full of soap, a man's shoe – but whatever had become of those others, the child was alone now, alone and mystified by the world around her, though not very much upset, by the time they came upon her. Maybe she had bawled out all her fear and grief and anger before then – for who knew how long she had been on that raft – but whatever her history, when Martin Jenner, the youngest of the boat's crewmen, got down off the *Chloë* and went to pick her up, she barely reacted. She just let herself be taken aboard (Martin still tells how badly she smelled, and how pretty she was) and brought back to Havergey, where she is still our youngest citizen. They called her Chloë, of course. She's six now. She has no memory at all of her parents, which may be for the best.'

*

Ben left me at four-thirty. By then, I thought I'd be glad to be alone for a while, to take stock, to listen to my blood ticking through my veins, to assess how much I was still suffering from the after-effects of my journey – but almost as soon as he was gone, I began to feel restless. I stood a while at the picture window, gazing out into the darkness, which had already settled in around the quarantine building, wondering if there was anything out there, any living thing that might be watching from the far edge of the meadow, or from the trees beyond, like that presence Max Jedermann had sensed at the ferry stop on his way home from India. Then, as odd as it might sound, the thought of Max made me feel lonely, all of a sudden and, though I wasn't conscious of doing so, I drifted over to the corner of the practice room that Ben had called 'the library' and pulled out the contents of The Archive once more. I think I was looking for something, though if I was, I didn't know what it was. Maybe I just wanted to hear another voice in my head, other than Ben's, or my own. Whatever the reason, I pulled out one of the large, clothbound notebooks, opened it at random, and began to read.

AUTOBIOGRAPHY OF
JOHN THE GARDENER

*Unfinished, found in a desk at Havergey House,
2045: Passage written June, 2026 (?)*

They used to tell us, back in Sunday School, that Heaven was an enormous room, a space that went on forever, where you never saw God, but you felt his presence, always. I liked that idea, back then, but now, if I had my way, I would have walls and divisions, hidden gardens steeped in gorgeous light, corridors leading off to secret rooms full of books or old toys. That way, you could wander from place to place, meeting your friends by chance, on an aimless walk through a meadow, or a woodland clearing full of foxgloves or daisies, remembering and forgetting and remembering again the faces of all the people you knew, and sometimes, in the long burn of a summer's day, coming through a stand of trees with the sense that someone is there, someone you can't see yet, though you know who it is, because your heart has guessed and by that guessing, made it so. The way it was in the early days with Chloë, when I didn't know it was her, coming towards me, except that I *knew* it was her – and there she was.

Now she is gone and all I have is a postcard, sent (c/o Mary) from southern Spain, when she was staying with her mother there, two years ago. She doesn't say much: The Guadalquivir is dry in its bed already, the Puente Romano is closed for restoration, just like last time, though it would seem that no work is actually being done. In the deep shade on Amador de los Rios, where she goes to escape her mother and the sun, a baby is walking step by slow step out of the darkness and into the sunlight that must seem, to him, so far away, his grandmother standing behind him, urging him on. 'Muy bien, muy bien.'

She was so far away. That was the hardest part of it. That I couldn't see her, or help her. Or no, that wasn't the hardest part: the hard part was that Hugh Follansbee sent her away and I still cannot be sure why he did it. Was it because of me? Did he want to separate us, because he thought we were getting too close? I've spoken to Max about this a few times, but he doesn't have a view about it – or nothing he will discuss with me. Still, he seems to sympathise, which surprises me, because at the time, when the plans were being made, and it was obvious neither Chloë nor her mother wanted to go, Max didn't try to intervene. Maybe he thought it wouldn't do any good – and he would have been right, probably. As far as Hugh Follansbee was concerned, everything here – the island, the gardens, the fish in the water, the people – *everything* was his to deal with as he saw fit. But then, by that time, I am sure, Max Jedermann either knew, or had begun to suspect, that Chloë wasn't Hugh Follansbee's daughter. I have no reason to be certain of this – he died before I ever plucked up the nous to ask him – but I think he knew and, if he knew, he also knew what spite there was in Hugh's decision. All I had was Chloë, and there was a time, I think, when I was her only true friend, if nothing more than that – and at the time all I could think was that Hugh Follansbee separated us, wilfully, just for spite.

That postcard was the last time I heard from Chloë. I can only surmise that she died in the first wave of the Great Epidemic of 2024, which killed hundreds of thousands along the Mediterranean coast in a matter of months – and that surprised me, because she had always seemed so protected, so *rich*. Not just in money, but in the various types of love her family and their friends could offer her: her mother's jaunty, almost sisterly affection, masking a deep conflict between wanting to protect this only daughter and let her go out into the world and be her own person, her father's wish to control everything around her, to keep her safe and intact – a desire to protect that drove a deliberate wedge between Chloë and me, not because there was anything untoward about our friendship (God help us, we were far too innocent for anything more untoward than a parting kiss, or occasional, glancing touches from which we withdrew a moment after). But then, that was about class, something I didn't understand till Chloë explained it, in one of the letters she used to leave for me in a gap in the wall of the Rose Garden, letters in which she allowed herself to be wiser than her seventeen years – and so, almost infinitely wiser than me, a boy of nineteen with, as Chloë's Aunt Nathalie used to say, 'everything and nothing in his head'.

That family. Everything about them infuriated me, Chloë said, and I didn't even know it. Well, that was true, while she was here, but I knew it last year, when Hugh disappeared, just before the third wave of the Epidemic, the one that began with three cases in Kent, then reached as far as Shetland, killing over forty percent of the UK's population and leaving the entire country in chaos (did he know it was coming and just run, leaving us to our fate? But how could he have known?). Max had predicted this, but he had not predicted how widely the disease would spread. Or had he? Did he know all along, and resign himself to his fate? 'The earth must heal itself,' he had begun to say back when the population reached eight billion in 2024, just before the first signs of the Epidemic showed. 'Eight billion is too many.' He used to help me out, sometimes, in the glasshouse. He was interested in plant genetics, and especially in how we selected for colour, though I couldn't tell him anything, because that is something you *feel*, after a while, just from doing it. He would sit in the old broken down chair by the door, flicking ash on to his lapels and watch me working, but never far away from one of his favourite topics of conversation. Population. Loss of species. The poisoning of the oceans. It was all a touch grim and the others didn't want to listen to him, but I listened and, when I got the news about Chloë, I knew he was right. 'Seven billion, eight billion, nine before you can say Jack Robinson,' he would say. 'It's too many. What this planet needs is a good old-fashioned fever.'

Well, he said it with such relish, everybody thought it was some kind of grim joke. They didn't think he was serious – much less that he was right. So we carried on, blindly, into an age of superbugs and fatal errors in the production, supply and application of antibiotics and other medicines, and the people died, eventually in their millions, till the world's population – as far as it can be reasonably estimated now – fell to exactly what Max said it would. That estimate was two billion, though it could have been lower. Of course, after all those people died, in the space of just a few years, the land did prosper and, though it will probably take decades, the seas are healing. Max called it The Chernobyl Effect and when he said that, even I thought he was joking. But no: it seems that Chernobyl had once been a major nuclear power facility, but there had been an accident, leading to a catastrophic meltdown, and mass evacuation, in 1986. At first, people were allowed to return to their homes, but later the area was sealed off – and that was when some kind of miracle happened. It took some time – around thirty years – but soon the land began to recover, and then to thrive, so it was more alive, richer and more diverse than it had been before the disaster. Max would quote a scientist named Robert Baker, who had studied the ecology of Chernobyl almost thirty years after the accident. 'The countryside is beautiful,' Baker said. 'The animals and plants are in greater numbers now than if the reactor had not gone down. The ecosystem is as it was before humans started living out there – except for the radiation. It seems as though normal human activities associated with agrarian society are more destructive than the world's worst nuclear meltdown.'

Max would linger on this analysis – and I knew he felt not just the sadness of that but also the shame. Once, he had been a scientist himself, but he had given it up to pursue studies of his own. Life Studies, he called them, as if he were there just to paint. And yes, he did paint, but his life studies were something else, something that nobody ever got to see, or decipher, because they were written in code and he died before he could bring his work into a unified whole. All I ever knew was that it had something to do with what we mean when we say the word: *life*. What it is to be alive. What goes when something dies. The Scholar said that traditional science had barely scraped the surface of what life was, but that the secret, he knew, was there, to be observed, first in the words we used for life, or the soul, or the places where spirit pools and flows in a living body (*anima, pneuma, chi, chakra*). Most of all, we felt it every day, intuitively, whenever we encountered another living thing. We knew it, but we had no way of making it real, to ourselves or to one another. We dismissed the most essential facts of life as superstition, or metaphor – and that dismissal had allowed us to go on with the tragic adventure of industrialisation till we had passed way beyond the point of recovery. Everything would have to fall before a new world could begin. Nobody else could bear him, when he talked like this, but I listened, and I think, to some extent, I understood. And I thought, if it was given me to live and play some part in his work, I would preserve his papers, and his various drawings and notebooks, for those who might come in that future time, so they might finish his work, and understand what it was he was trying to say.

★

I broke off from my reading. John was rather dull, to be frank, and I didn't really want to read yet another story of lost love – I was beginning to feel a little squeamish and, if I am frank, I was aware of something in myself, some lack, or perhaps some cowardice, that had always prevented me from loving in that sad, lost way – the way John seemed to have loved Chloë, the way Max must have loved Paola. Still, the idea of a notebook full of coded writings on science intrigued me and, setting John the Gardener's book aside, I started going back through the items in The Archive, to see what I might have missed.

There was nothing. The coded books were gone – or they were being kept elsewhere. After all, much of this Archive's contents did consist of copies. Xeroxed, long ago, in some cases, when the estate still had a copier that worked. Some were hand-copied in a dark, sepia-coloured ink (the ink that, now, I am using to write this, even though I have almost abandoned any plan to try to get this report back to 2017). Maybe the coded files were too complicated to copy. Maybe they were too precious. I hoped the Havergeyans had kept them, that they were in a safe place in the 'big house', as Ben called it. That way, I might get to see them one day – and maybe, if I could decode them, I might discover something useful, something that might justify my future residence to those who were already at home on the island.

QUARANTINE

I slept fitfully, and woke before dawn. Something was bothering me, some nagging thought at the back of my head that I had missed something, something obvious, but important, and I went back out to The Archive and began unpacking it again. One thing I had noticed was that the 'autobiography' of John the Gardener was very long, which seemed suspicious to me. What did this man, a gardener who had never left the island as far as I could tell, what story, other than the most obvious one, could he possibly have to tell? I began flicking through the three notebooks that comprised his life story, looking for any sign that, for safety's sake, or to keep them secret from someone he didn't want to know about them, he had concealed Max Jedermann's coded writings among his own. But there was nothing. Page after page, there was nothing but notes about the garden, sad memories of Chloë (he had even written a few poems, though I couldn't get past the first few lines) and reminiscences of an extremely pedestrian childhood. Elsewhere, I was just as unlucky. Other than notebooks, the various images and some large folders of ephemera – menus, bills, catalogues, even theatre programmes from the twentieth century – there was nothing that looked like code, however crude. Finally, I gave up and went back to bed. Almost the moment I fell asleep, however, Ben arrived and, though I could tell he was trying to let me lie, moving quietly below as he set out the breakfast things, I couldn't get back to sleep, so I got up, put on the dressing gown he had brought me – elegant, in a grey Japanese kimono style – and went down to join him.

*

Ben had really pushed the boat out. In my old life – I was already thinking of it that way, which shocked me a little – I had never been much for breakfasts. A cup of tea, a slice of toast. Coffee and a doughnut. It depended where I was. Now, though, I watched in fascination as he prepared the coming feast – and I couldn't wait. However, I was in just as much of a hurry to know more about the material I had been reading overnight, and I didn't think it would be inappropriate to start talking about it while he finished setting out the little delicacies he had brought along to enhance our breakfast table. 'I've been reading John the Gardener's book,' I said. 'The autobiography.'

'Good.'

'It's all quite – poignant –'

'Yes, it is.'

'He and Max, they were both unlucky in love,' I said. 'It seemed like an odd parallel – both of them losing the women they loved because of Hugh Follansbee's meddling.'

Ben nodded. 'Yes,' he said. 'Those stories are – sad…' He seemed not to be very engaged with stories, however. He was thinking about something else.

'So what happened to John?' I said.

Ben frowned. 'We think John the Gardener died around 2040. Not, as it happened, from one of the several viruses that had raged through the land several times in the previous years. In fact, he outlived the Great Epidemic, which had lasted, on and off, from the first wave that killed Chloë in 2024 until around 2032, when one final, but virulent strain of influenza killed millions all across Europe, including John's young wife and his little daughter. We estimate, from his book (in which, rather strangely for a work that calls itself an autobiography, he does not give his date of birth) that he was around forty-two when he died – of natural causes, as it happened. Of course, he may have been weakened by the years of disease his body had somehow resisted when others did not, and he had experienced more than his fair share of grief. In the space of eight years, John's world had been unpeopled. As he buried the last of his neighbours he must have wondered if he was the last person in the world. Finally, he was alone. It would seem that, sometime during that final wave of disease, all contact with the mainland had stopped, and John assumes, wrongly as it turned out, that everyone there had also died out. So, it seemed to him, that the whole world had become a Chernobyl: all human activity ceased, and the land returning to its original wildness.

'Ah. I can see that you are becoming impatient. There's something else you want to know.' He smiled. 'By the way, you must tell me, sometime, about that place you came from, and what happened to you there that makes you so very interested in romance stories. You know, of course, that – as long as this quarantine works out, which seems likely – you are welcome to stay on Havergey for as long as you wish. I suspect you have no other options, but we'd rather, if you stayed, that you did so by choice. One thing I would say, with some degree of conviction, is that you won't be going back to 2017. I don't doubt that time is not a linear phenomenon, my friend, but the calendar is. The clock is. If you came here from 2017 –'

'If?'

He smiled. 'If you came here from the past, then you have found a way to cheat the calendar, but I'm not sure what your position is with regard to time. Still, I'll just assume that the odd blue box out there is some kind of literary device. That way, I can allow myself the odd literary device of my own. We're all friends here – and if you can't say that here, in our little Utopia, Beta Version, where can you say it?'

'I told you before,' I said. 'I'm not one of those – *Utopia People*. And what do you mean by literary device? You saw for yourself – Tardis B is real –'

'I saw you get out,' he said. 'I didn't see you arrive –'

'Well, I didn't arrive,' I said. 'I mean, not in space –'

'That blue box wasn't there four days ago.'

'I know,' I said. 'Isn't that the point?'

'It's all right,' he said. 'There's nothing to get angry about. I'm just trying to – get my head around what's going on. Here you are, come from nowhere, and… Well, we've all read the books. You get to Utopia, or something like it, by having a dream, or building a time machine. William Morris – *A*

Dream of John Ball, H.G. Wells, Ray Bradbury – *The Toynbee Convector*. Thing is, did you come here in that blue box, or are you dreaming now? And is this Utopia? That, in the end, will be for you to judge – all I can say is that, for us, Utopia, or something like it, is two discernible steps away from any place where people are healthy and determined enough to take those steps. The first step is preparation. What happened on Havergey, after Hugh Follansbee was out of the picture, was an effort – though not necessarily a conscious one – at preparation for Utopia. First, on the part of John the Gardener, and then by the people who came here later – nomads of the first wave, and now, apparently, of the old order. All I can tell you about Utopia is how to prepare for it. After that, the question of whether it has truly come into existence can only be answered by its inhabitants, and it can only be true on a temporary basis. Things are always changing, and today's paradise might well be tomorrow's prison. As a wanderer on Havergey, I would say that this is the most holy place I have ever seen, and I know the others who live here feel the same way, or they would have moved on years ago. That would make complete sense – we did begin as nomads, after all.' He took a deep breath. 'Sorry,' he said. 'Sometimes I talk too much. Let's rest our heads for a while and have some more tea. Then, maybe, if you think it might help, we can talk about The Creation Myth.'

He stood up. 'Same again?'

I nodded.

'I brought quite a range today,' he said. 'Ceylon, Lapsang, green tea. One day it will all run out, but for now...' His voice faded away, and he turned a little to see better what had just caught his eye outside the window. I sat up and looked out. Out in the grey light, over the snow, a doe was passing the window, with three younger deer following and, though there was no logical reason to think so, I felt they were aware of us, even behind the window. Or was it just the light that had attracted them? Ben grinned. 'That's a good omen,' he said.

'Of what?'

He shook his head and filled the kettle. 'No idea,' he said. 'Maybe for our conversation.' He was old school in his way of making tea, it reminded me of my mother. Usually, I just tossed a bag into a mug and poured hot water over it, but with Ben it was like some kind of tea ceremony. Everything was deliberate, slow. Finally, when it was all done, he brought the pot and some fresh teacups to the table.

'Do you remember, I told you that The Creation Myth is derived entirely from The Archive you have been studying so closely?' He smiled – ironically, I thought. He was clearly amused by my interest in the island's former inhabitants and their personal lives. 'Well, I wasn't being quite accurate. Every person on Havergey brought something to the myth, and for a while it was constantly being amended.' He gave me a meaningful look. 'Maybe it will be you who makes the next amendment. I'm sure you have things to add – '

I shook my head. 'I'm not really the philosophical type,' I said. 'I'm more – theoretical.'

'Ah.' He nodded. 'Though I have to say, the Myth is more practical, in many ways, than it is philosophical. It's like Emma Goldman said: "A revolution without dancing is not a revolution worth having."'

I smiled. I'd heard that quote before, in a slightly different form.

'Still,' Ben continued. 'Even though we brought our own experiences, our own choreographies to Havergey, The Creation Myth was constructed, in theory, from these papers and artefacts, and most of those who now enjoy life on Havergey not only hold this botched narrative dear, but have got parts of it down by heart and will not so much repeat as extemporise on it on a winter's night when the cold stills the land outside, or on long walks by the river when they are transporting goods from one place to another. Of course, to some it will seem odd, and perhaps a touch grandiose, to call this narrative of ours a creation myth – but it is, in its way, the story of how the new Havergey, so very different from the old Havergey, came into being and, if a new place comes into being, surely it deserves a creation myth of its own.' He looked at me – to see, I think, how interested I was in all of this. 'As I said, it isn't so much a story of origin as a set of principles, a set of – precepts. That sounds too grand, though, and we don't want that. In a way, the Havergey we dwell in today happened by accident, a tragic accident, you might say, but if you look at it from a different perspective, it doesn't seem accidental at all – and that, I suppose, is the first of the precepts.'

He stopped talking and looked at me expectantly. So much had been going through my head, after his outburst on time machines and dreams, that I didn't know what to say. Maybe he had been right and I was dreaming, after all. Maybe I had lost consciousness in the Tardis and I was still there, having this dream. But then, if this was a dream, could I propose to myself, within the frame of that dream, that I was only dreaming? I felt a little sick. 'What precept?' I managed, finally.

He smiled. 'That everything is governed by grace. I have spoken about this before, but I don't think I have ever said what we mean by it – partly because to do so isn't easy. We can say, for now, that a human being is in a state of grace when he or she is in accord with Tao, with – nature naturing. When he sees what is there, and not what he wants to be there. When he does not try to impose his will upon events, but moves in accord with the overall – '

'Go with the flow,' I said. I remembered that. I'd never heard it used other than ironically. Usually with the word 'man' at the end. As in –

'No,' Ben said. 'That old bullshit is – bullshit. Because that was just a cop-out, an abuse of the *wu wei* principle so as to do nothing at all. Passivity. *Wu wei* doesn't mean inaction, it means *just* action *when it is called for* – and to know when action is called for, you have to be constantly alert. You have to be an accomplished watcher. *Wu wei* is the very opposite of that go with the flow *laissez-faire* mentality. To practise *wu wei* is to be *in* the flow, to work alongside the emergent, to see the antithesis that naturally arises to balance out the thesis, the *yin* that arises to complement the *yang*, and to be alert to all the forces and energies and elements that are all working at once, to find or to overthrow balance.'

He looked at me and I nodded, to show that I understood.

'But remember, balance is always temporary. Provisional. Something is always in play – as soon as balance is achieved, something new happens, there's a shift – and this is, in fact, natural, because if what we think of as balance was to become permanent it would end in entropy. On the one hand, chaos, on the other entropy – we're not talking physics here, by the way – '

'It would seem a bit odd if we were,' I said.

He smiled. 'But you see what I am saying. *Yin* and *yang*, thesis and antithesis, it's all about play. It's not a matter of competing forces, it's about complementarities. A balancing act in which everything is constantly in motion, constantly playing, just as you are – that play of the in-breath and the out-breath that is constantly defining you as individual, then balancing that with the fact that you cannot exist as that individual unless you bring him into play... Every moment is a balancing act and so every moment, every breath sequence, in and out, is a pursuit of what is *just*, because justice is balance, but balance doesn't mean stillness, for that would be – '

I smiled. 'Entropy?'

He nodded.

'We're really *not* talking about physics here,' I said.

'No, because none of what I am saying refers to a closed system.' He gave me a long look; he wasn't smiling now. 'This is a real world.'

I didn't feel any need to argue.

'But that's really neither here nor there,' he said. 'Real and not real, like beautiful and ugly, even they are complementarities. What matters is the play between them. And that's why we say: *In the beginning was the breath.* And the breath was play. Each moment, an improvisation – and with each breath, I make that play between myself and the world into a story, a story that I call me. Me, myself. Me and you. I and thou. A story. We can be fooled into thinking that story is real, or true, or mine and yours, or mine alone. Or we can see the play together and, even though nothing changes that we can describe or name, everything changes. You don't know what I am talking about, do you?'

I laughed. 'Absolutely no idea,' I said. 'It all sounds very…'

'Mystical?' He grinned. 'It's not. It couldn't be less so. Still, the Havergey we know now really began to exist on the day the Scholar taught John the Gardener to meditate. It was meditation that brought this Havergey of ours into being – and meditation is the key idea of The Creation Myth. Everyone who lives on Havergey practises a very simple form of meditation, one that is very difficult to learn. What is interesting about any discipline is that it brings different gifts to each of its practitioners: when I learned to meditate, for example, I immediately saw that the breath was the basic ground of this universal play I've been talking about. With the in-breath, you take in the world; with the out-breath, you release yourself to the world. This is echoed in the first steps a child takes, if it is raised with love: because, as Ian D. Suttie says…' He closed his eyes and took a deep breath. "The Baby-Mother bond is vaguely and intuitively appreciated by the former as mutual absorption. By degrees the baby's expanding activities and sense-impressions change the character of this bond. A service rendered to the baby's body and a caress are originally indistinguishable by it, but the baby's perceptions of and interest in its own body and its immediate surroundings grow rapidly under the influence of the mother's ministrations. In this way it develops Interest-in-Itself, the process Freud misconceives as Narcissism. It is of course arbitrary to say at what point the companionship of love becomes the companionship of interest, but there is no doubt that the feeling-relationship of the companions does change as attention ceases to be absorbed wholly and reciprocally each in the other and becomes directed convergently to the same things. Cooperative activities, identical or complementary attitudes to outside happenings, build up a world of common meanings which marks a differentiation from simple love wherein 'the world' of each is the other person. The simple direct bond has become a triangular relationship wherein external objects form the medium of play." He breathed deeply again and smiled. 'I memorised that years ago, and I still remember it all. Sometimes I worry that I'll forget the parts of The Archive that I got by heart, but so far, so good. Anyhow, what matters most is Suttie's conclusion.'

'Which is?'

'That "necessity is not the mother of invention; play is." He smiled and I nodded; it was a pleasing idea, though I didn't know if it was actually true.

'Does that sound too optimistic?' he said.

'Maybe.'

'Well, I would argue that I'm not an optimist. I'm just someone who believes we should be prepared. For good things as much as for bad.' He drained what was left of his tea. 'This is one of those seven-cup mornings, isn't it?' he said.

'It's getting that way,' I said.

He detected the irony in my voice, but he only smiled. It seemed the lesson for today was over. Or almost, at least. 'Anyhow,' he said. 'For me, this is Havergey's main gift, that it is founded upon the play of the breath. In-breath, out-breath, the illusion of the inner self and the illusion of the objective world, constantly balancing one another. Havergey's gift to me was this: to breathe fully, playfully, effortlessly. For me, everything is embodied in that play of breath – even the community itself. After all, the basis of any community is the spirit its founders brought to a particular place, and how long they maintained it. History shows that this spirit can be distorted by any number of factors: it takes a really robust community not to become competitive, not to grow factions, not to allow itself to become compromised by the desire for property, especially as a population grows – and this is why I say that we can only prepare for Utopia, because the best we shall achieve, *over time*, is an ever-shifting and provisional approximation. Only the moment is perfect. This is one of the tenets of the nomads who came here and began their work where John the Gardener and the Scholar left off. Understand that only the moment is perfect. Be prepared, in all your dealings with the world, to experience each moment as it happens. This has nothing to do with wealth, or status, or wisdom, in the usual sense. It doesn't even have very much to do with happiness. Or not as we used to understand it. We would always ask: can one be happy, if others are not? Of course, there is no question in this. But can one be happy if others are denied the *basis* for happiness? If others are being held in ignorance, for example? Happiness is not a thing, it's not a piece of property. I don't *have* it, I experience it. But I can't give it to another person. I can't make you happy. All I can do is tell you what I learned that led to me being open to happiness. This is true of everything. Every gift and every curse. We should not be confused into treating them differently.'

THE SCHOLAR'S BOOK

Was it a coincidence that, as soon as Ben left and I returned to my reading, the first thing I saw echoed what he had just been saying to me? Back then, I would have said, Yes, of course it was, but I have lived in Havergey for some months now, and there is something about the place that makes questions like that more complicated than they seem at first sight. Once again, I had opened S03 to a random page. It seemed to me that the Scholar was older now and The Collapse may have begun – I couldn't be sure, because there were no dates.

*

There is surely nothing other than the single purpose of the present moment. A man's whole life is a succession of moment after moment. There will be nothing else to do, and nothing else to pursue. Live being true to the single purpose of the moment.

THE BOOK OF HAGAKURE

The test, in middle age, is to be gracious to your former self – the one who, with his extreme appetite, near absence of critical thinking, or sheer perversity, fouled everything up. Youth is wasted on the young, as they say. The test, after that, is to keep up the necessary maintenance, so that you can finally pay attention to the world in itself. During this phase, there is no greater gift than *l'Autre*.

Dear Paola

I'm sitting in a hotel room in Munich at five in the morning, sleepless, not unhappy and certainly not depressed, though maybe suspended, somewhat, between one state and another, the shadows gathered round, yes, but oddly neutral, so it feels like some kind of truce, some limited but adequate peace has been achieved between my ghost of a body and the night's slow unwinding. The hotel is next to the English Gardens and, through the open window, I hear its various birds, a wandering net of conversation and appeal that runs from the sycamores and silver limes at this edge of the park to the awakening city beyond. I was out last night but I didn't join in the usual bacchanal – or not enough to make me sleep, at least, which I regretted later because, for some time now, the only sure path to sleep has been alcohol or drugs or both, and I am reminded once more that, for some of us, it's the better angels of our being who cause the most trouble, just as I understand, at the very back of my mind, that sleeplessness is a trouble worth having, a gift of sorts, to counteract the inattention of the daytime.

Well, you know better than anyone that I'm not one of those people who gets sentimental about company. I like being far from home (and these days, home is a very debatable land indeed), sitting quietly in a bare room listening to the dark.

But this morning, for some reason, I think it would be good to
go downstairs and find my old friend from the most luxurious
of lonely childhoods waiting for me in the lobby in his hat and
coat, or sitting in the breakfast room, with fresh coffee, and
maybe a rumba playing on an old-fashioned gramophone
in the corner, blocking out everything while he sifts random
consolations from moonlight on a row of dustbins, or from
the fog of a harbour dawn, leaning, for one last moment, on
a cold window sill. You remember? How we used to read
Hart Crane in bed, back in Cambridge and Pisa, in what
you liked to call our illicit days? Now that everyone is gone
– or so it seems to me, with Felix and Tiziana in prison,
and dear Yvonne dead from this… But maybe I am being
presumptuous. Maybe not everyone is gone from you. Maybe
you have found new – friends, I would have written but, to be
truthful, the old recidivist in me was picturing something else
entirely. I cannot say how much that shames me, that I picture
you with someone else and can even begin to want to deny you
that happiness.

'Chaplinesque' was the first poem I 'got' of his. Do
you remember? It's the one that begins 'We make our meek
adjustments…' And indeed we do. We don't want to and
sometimes we're even brave about it, but more often than not
there's compromise because, much of the time, 'the world' is
too huge and too insistent on taking the least interesting path
between two points. By which I mean, the moneyed world,
the social order, smug Hugh Follansbee's world – whatever
people are calling that these days. For my part, I think of that
Authorised Version of vulgar rule where the goalposts are
always in motion and the lies are so blatant it seems pointless
to contest them. I mean, I think of everything bad now as
Brother Hugh's world. Or I did, until –

We make our meek adjustments… And there's nothing

new in that, except that right now, we're so good at meek adjustment that we barely know we're doing it. All the shit we've complained about for years – for decades – all the lies and the bankers ripping us off again and the government pissing away our moral standing on far-off wars, the complete abandonment of the principles, if not the rhetoric, of social justice – and we just shake our heads, dismayed, but not surprised, our meek adjustments robotically clicking in, over and over again. Is it because there's so much consolation in art, so much beauty in dustbins and lonely, moonlit alleys, or have we just settled for consolations that, in some previous era, would have shamed us to the quick? I'm sorry, I'm becoming incoherent, from lack of sleep, I suppose and –

Oh, Hart Crane, Hart Crane… I loved him so much but then I tired of lyric resignation and his dream of a passing moment that is really not much more than the peace of the fathers and I got angry, to no real end. And I still think it's not enough: surely, there are better choices to be made and, as persuasive as the little tramp might be in the world of metaphor, it's time now for the spirit of Buster Keaton to rise up and lead us all down the less travelled road – inventive, anarchic, potentially fatal – that Hart Crane walked only for as long as he was able, wildly, desperately perhaps, and with the thick slide of the rumba somewhere in his bones as he sat alone, in a hotel lobby, scribbling verses on a lime-stained napkin, his face bright with dawn and attention and the notion, however fleeting, that a just rhythm could still make some difference in the world. It's almost enough, and it's not enough; because soon, maybe now, while the meek adjustments continue to be made, the epigraph he chose for White Buildings, *a single line from Rimbaud, that most Keatonesque of poets, will rise, salty and razor-sharp on the wind:* 'Ce ne peut être que la fin du monde, en avançant.'

*Dearest Paola! You always said I made more sense when
I was drunk, or high. Now I'm just bitter and vengeful, and
I make no sense at all. By now, you will have heard about
Felix and the others – and maybe you have jumped to a
conclusion so terrifying I can't even bear to think about it. In
fact, I can't think about it, because I don't have the words – I
don't even have... Do you remember, you said the language
was incomplete if it has no word for how that hare stood,
so upright, caught in the beam of our headlamps and how
it turned to us, as if to face us down? You remember? I said
it had no word for whatever it was lingered in my hands
when I washed away the smoke after a bonfire, and you said,
there was no word to describe the shape in your head that
continued after all the bells stop, all over the village, all at
once? Now all I can say is that there is no word for how I
feel, not just the injustice of what has happened to the others
but also of the idea that you might think...*

*I didn't know what to think, at first. I was just waiting
for someone to come for me. But they didn't – and that
was the first clue. They didn't come for me, because Yvonne
protected me. She could do nothing for Felix, it seems –
though now I know the whole story, now that she and
Chloë are also gone, I see why. She could do nothing for
Felix because he was the main target. Because – how, I will
never know – Brother Hugh found out about them. But
how? Was it Chloë? Did she tell him, after she found those
letters – letters I had meant to destroy? Letters I couldn't
destroy because they were all I had left of you. I didn't even
remember that we'd talked about Felix and Yvonne – I
thought we were always so safely absorbed in our own story.
But I must have mentioned something somewhere – and I
should have guessed Chloë would find those letters and read
them because that was her nature.*

So, there it is. In our different ways, we were all betrayed – and it was Brother Hugh, I'm sure of it. First he sent Yvonne and Chloë away (poor John, our love-struck gardener: he thought Chloë had been packed off to Europe to get her away from him). Then Brother Hugh passed on whatever he knew about Felix to the authorities – I can see him now, building a file, putting two and two together. We were so careless, especially considering the times we were in. It wasn't a game any more, by that time, you couldn't play at politics. Just a word, a whisper, a sign – that was enough to damn the most innocent of dreamers.

Now, I will make Hugh pay for his treachery. I say this quite calmly, and without anger. I don't feel a need for vengeance – I know that will not bring anything back that was lost. But there is one factor that outweighs everything else, and that is honour. For honour's sake – which, in the end, is for the sake of all, including Hugh – I must make him appreciate the depth of the harm he has done, and give him his opportunity to make amends

*

The letter breaks off there. There is no way of knowing if Max ever finished it, though I am fairly certain he didn't send it. It would have been too incriminating. I say this because, in 2025, presumably around the time this letter was composed, Hugh Follansbee disappeared. Officially, it was believed that he had travelled to America, for fear that the epidemic that had killed his wife and daughter would come to Havergey next – but I don't think that is what he did. I think Max found a way of making 'Brother Hugh' pay for his sins, and that the old tyrant of Havergey lies somewhere in its grounds, probably deep in the orchard, or in the West Wood, feeding the thistles and the starry masterworts that he once made such efforts to kill off, when he was lord of Havergey for a day.

What is really striking, however, is the fact that, if I am right, and Max really did kill his brother-in-law, he was as calm as he said he was, because after a day, or a few days, or at most a week, he continued writing in his commonplace book, as if nothing had happened.

★

At times you have to create – or allow, or perhaps collaborate with – disorder to get to the place where the 'real' work appears to begin. At times you must create order, no matter how artificial, to prepare the way for a new chaos. These are always different events, even if they use the same 'materiel', but they are also continuous, no matter how large or clear the spaces between seem to be.

Because I'd been asleep, I didn't know the train had already reached the old heartland. Not, I admit, a term that geographers would recognise; but *heartland*, nonetheless. Typical features include: derelict houses perched along the banks of grey canals, the brickwork stained with smoke and damp, the crumbling mortar sprouting toadflax or buddleja; four grey horses out to pasture, always four: they have been there for decades and will never be reclaimed. The church at the edge of its village, no longer the property of God. The implausible beauty of disused mineheads, last traces of an industrial-surreal that fell out of fashion so soon it might never have happened. The mainstream texts inform us that this heartland is an illusion, but you only have to look to see that it's not a dream at all and, worse still, that some old god is out there, patient as a lost child, waiting for someone he can trust to walk him home.

Vicious eye gouger of legend, winged shadow from a superstitious childhood, a low buzzard scours the upland pastures, searching for the newborn and the weak. Ever since my special day with Hugh, I like them better than most humans.

What I want from a painting is the blue of certain deserts at certain times, the blue of empty strand or tundra, a blue that only the most perfect instruments could register, a blue that signals the end of all the usual jurisdictions.

Freedom as the recognition of necessity? Always – but who could have guessed how much grace there would be in the enactment?

The question of presence does not apply only to the Christian god. Any god who could somehow be considered present (or real, or made flesh) immediately becomes less powerful. What renders a god omnipotent is the fact of his absence.

Here, the local gods have no use for trinkets. They lie down in the earth till summer comes, then steal from yard to yard, while the townsfolk are busy eating, or making love, behind closed doors: bear-shapes, rat-shapes, shapes we only see in nightmares. Best are the ones that straggle in from the woods with thumbprints of light in their fur, like hieroglyphs, or the lost names for things we have forgotten. The grass that used to run through here for miles; the last of the blackberries, fly-blown and sweet as molasses.

It's never what we wanted, happiness. What's most confusing is the notion that it ought to be more or less permanent, some lifelong Reich of *dolce vita*. Add to that the fear that it is not really happiness, but mere pleasure in disguise, and it is not surprising that almost nobody has mastered the discipline of lingering on the grace-filled moment for as long, but only for as long, as it lasts.

Hope is a thing with feathers. No. It's just a bird we bring in from the cold after it breaks its wing on the picture window. We tend it lovingly, it fades. This is altogether natural and only a fool would think of it as sentimentalism, on the one hand, or tragedy, on the other.

School-book science: an abridged version of natural history that fails to take account of tenderness.

What Sigmund Freud didn't know about love would fill several volumes.

Thinking of Felix today. Of what an ideologue he is. He never understood that we also have to cure ourselves of ideology, which is nothing more than an extension of property.

There's a film in my mind, but I don't know if it's one I have seen at the cinema, or composed in my head. There's really only one scene that I remember completely: the windows are daubed with rain and *noir*, another cinematic night pressed to the glass, while someone is driving away in a white Corvette.

This feels like a conclusion. But then, we do well to remember the first rule of B-movie psychology: that, for ninety percent of the playing time, you are in the original movie, but the last ten percent – the part where it no longer seems that the world is just about to vanish – was probably tacked on afterwards by the studio.

On the other hand, one image is all the proof anyone could need that having loved not wisely, but with just the right amount of narrative, is possibly the most you can ever dare to hope for.

'Heaven' is local now. Fresh rain damping the gravel in the yard, sunlit trees and the crab apples waiting to fall. I wonder why anyone ever thought the sky was larger than a garden? Why anyone would need a guide or a herald to lead them through a field of Queen Anne's lace to where the light begins as elsewhere?

Visit the sick. Bring them books and flowers. But always remember that, to them, nothing you have to offer is better than morphine.

The light of the public with which you yourself collaborate (actor, performer) is like a trapdoor through which, innocently, you fall into a place so ugly, you could not possibly have imagined it.

There are those who say you have to risk hell to avoid purgatory. For myself, not understanding such propositions, I loiter at the gates of *l'autre monde* (Heaven, if you will) pretending not to know where I am.

It would be meaningless to say, I am the Great Spirit. But to say that the Great Spirit is separate from me is to misunderstand the nature of being.

Sidereal time belongs to the dead. Calendar time to the undead (Nabokov: 'There is many a person whose soul has gone to sleep like a leg.') The creaturely life unfolds in seasonal time.

In theory, one could be happy. The principle is simple: to be happy, one has only to live in the eternal present. This is an easy piece of theoretical knowledge to acquire, and can be found in most of the major religions and life philosophies, in one form or another.

In practice, however, something quite improbable has to happen before one can even commence with the discipline of happiness. An abandonment that, unless one is prepared to withdraw entirely from 'the world', must be maintained in the most inventive ways and against all kinds of subtle opposition. And, of course, happiness, when one has entered into that discipline, is nothing like one's idea of what happiness would be, in the days before the abandonment. Because what we abandon is exactly the state of mind in which the false terms of happiness are defined.

William Morris: 'The true secret of happiness lies in taking a genuine interest in all the details of daily life.'

Every death is a gift to the next generation. To the extent that we are wise, that gift is made, not just willingly, but wholeheartedly. Our regeneration depends upon that generosity of spirit.

I have at least lived long enough to realise that I had spent far too long congratulating myself on simply surviving the condition of having a character like mine.

I remember Chloë at the Edinburgh Botanics on Linnaeus Day. How old was she then? She came home with a head full of names and a sense that the world has suddenly clicked into place. *Pinus. Cotinus. Linnaea.* Another way of seeing, like the early days of learning colour words. Another sifting of the world, another stratum of order.

Old John used to say he could see the fairies still, from time to time. It embarrassed Young John terribly, but that's because he didn't understand what his father means by 'fairies'. Or so I presume to think. How it seems to me now is that the old man caught glimpses of something that belongs to this place – the *genius loci*, say, or that darker spirit, the *genius cucullatus*, that even hardened Roman infantrymen believed in, that spirit native to wild land and forests – the only places that the Romans, with their termini and their straight roads, feared. Old John saw that spirit only in certain kinds of weather, in autumn, say, through gusts of falling beech leaves, and he was looking at it all as if through a veil – because he was *looking*. He wanted to see something that matched some kind of expectation, a single, local form, not something he knew was impossible. So he saw – fairies, the way he saw selkies on the shore, or kelpies, or any of those other supernatural creatures that are, in fact, just facets of that one spirit, that one energy – the genius of the place, which is more physical than we thought it was, even though it can never be grasped, or fully pictured, or captured in the mind.

The appropriate action, the just action, would have to be independent of its consequences.

The old cliché – one crime begets another. It took a long time to take the final step, but it is done. Still, I think of Yamamoto: 'When one has made a decision to kill a person, even if it will be very difficult to succeed by advancing straight ahead, it will not do to think about doing it in a long, roundabout way. One's heart may slacken, he may miss his chance, and by and large there will be no success. The Way of the Samurai is one of immediacy, and it is best to dash in headlong.'

★

I had to stop there. Not just because I was tired, but because it felt like witnessing a confession. And not just any confession, but the confession of a man who is gradually losing his grip on reality. Had the others seen this? Had Ben? Max, the sage, Max, the Scholar – Max the lunatic. He had lost everything and, by now I was convinced of it, he had killed his enemy, in cold blood, as a matter of honour. Did nobody else see that?

QUARANTINE

After that last dip into Max's books, I had trouble sleeping that night. The image of the Scholar doing away with Hugh Follansbee haunted me, though I couldn't imagine how he had accomplished the deed. For some reason, I had pictured 'Brother Hugh' as a substantial person, a big, or at least a heavy man, not somebody it would be easy to overcome. Whereas Max – well, the Max in the photographs looked fit and fairly limber, but he seemed slight and there was nothing in his face that would suggest an ability to kill. In fact, he seemed to me, as his nickname suggested, a quiet, bookish man, gentle and slightly withdrawn, one who preferred the company of women – his sister, his niece, Paola – to men. On the other hand, nowhere was it stated that he had actually killed Hugh. It was only implied – and implied, at that, in the writings of a man now half-mad. Where, for that matter, was the body? I lay all night thinking about these questions; then, when Ben arrived next day with the breakfast things,

I couldn't wait to ask him what he knew, and I plunged straight into something akin to an interrogation, as soon as he'd poured the tea.

'I've been reading,' I said. 'I found a letter from Max Jedermann –'

Ben nodded. He seemed quite unperturbed. 'Ah, yes,' he said. 'You found that.'

'Yes.'

'Interesting, isn't it?'

'I don't know,' I said. 'If what he says is true –'

'We'll never know,' Ben said, cracking open a boiled egg.

'Well,' I said. 'Does anybody actually know what happened to Follansbee?' I asked.

Ben looked at me. 'I assume Max Jedermann killed him,' he said. 'That's what the book seems to be saying. And the fact that he didn't actually send the letter does suggest –'

'How do you know he didn't send it? The letter in the notebook could have been a draft. Or a copy.'

Ben shook his head. 'No,' he said, 'We know. Elaine and Margaret, the Wilson sisters – you'll meet them, they're identical twins, always together, can't stand to be apart, finish each other's sentences, that kind of thing. Well, they did all the research, really. It seems Paola died in the same wave of disease that killed Yvonne and Chloë. We know that Max had tried writing to her several times, but the letters came back return to sender. Finally, he guessed but, as you see, he kept on writing to her, on occasion –'

'It seems to me he was starting to lose his mind.'

'Very possible.'

'And you are sure he actually did kill Hugh?'

VII

'I see no reason to doubt it.'

'But that doesn't bother you?' I said. I was beginning to feel a little exasperated. 'I mean, it doesn't trouble you, that your Scholar, the man whose books this whole community is based upon, was probably a murderer?'

Ben considered this for a moment. Then he took a sip of tea. 'Well, I'd say he was more of a killer. With good reasons to kill, no?'

'It's still killing.'

Ben smiled grimly. 'It is,' he said. 'But then, Hugh effectively murdered four people. Worse, really. He sent them to – God knows what torture and misery. He's hardly an innocent.'

'Interesting views for a pacifist.'

He laughed. 'I suppose so,' he said. 'But remember, everything you read in the notebooks is a story. Told from one or another person's point of view. Max. John. Chloë's delightful attempt at a topographical study –'

I hadn't found this yet. 'Chloë?' I said.

'You haven't read that?' he said. 'Well, you ought to read it. It's a shambles, but charming. She wrote it when she discovered she wasn't Hugh's daughter, after all. It's not finished, sadly, but it gives another perspective on what the old Havergey was like, before the tyranny ended.' He poured some more tea for himself. 'Would you like some?' he asked.

I nodded. 'So Hugh was a tyrant, who had to die.'

Ben nodded. 'That's it,' he said, with a happy smile. 'Sometimes it's the only way. After all, as the Scholar says, "why waste mercy?"' He poured me some more tea and I could smell it, that sweet, grassy scent. 'But enough of all this,' he said. 'Why don't you tell me a story about yourself.'

'A story?'

'Nothing with love in it,' he said. 'And I assume you don't have any murders in your past – '

'I don't have much of a past at all,' I said.

He laughed. 'Pick something at random,' he said. 'Things like that, they're usually more interesting than you think.'

I thought. This was silly, I told myself, but then a memory came into my mind and, for no reason that I could have given then, it felt like a story – or not a story, really, just an anecdote – that I wanted to tell. But I couldn't figure out how to begin.

Ben nodded, as if he'd read my mind. 'Take your time,' he said. 'Have some tea.'

I took a sip of the tea he had just poured. It was hot. 'Well,' I said. 'I suppose it's a good thing that I went into time travel – at least it doesn't involve too much navigation.' I stopped talking, and he smiled encouragingly. I tried again. 'When I was young, there were so many places I wanted to see. Like Lake Baikal. I always wanted to walk the Great Baikal Trail. All around that part of the world. To cross Mongolia on horseback. To see the Great Steppe. To stand, alone and quiet, in a Siberian forest. Oh, and I almost managed to get myself sent to Antarctica.'

Ben laughed. 'Why did you want to go to Antarctica?'

'I don't know,' I said. 'Just to see. But I didn't get to go, so I took some time off and drove across the United States on Route 50. Do you know it?'

He gave me a blank look. 'Where is it?' he said.

'It runs from Ocean City, Maryland, to Sacramento, California. All the way across the US, going through thirteen states, and barely one major city in all that way.'

'So, what do you remember about it?' Ben said. 'I mean, what's the story?'

I nodded. I was beginning to see it all clearly. 'Well,' I said. 'In the one memory that's really clear, I'm about halfway through the journey. It's a warm, late October afternoon in east Kansas. I'm maybe twenty or thirty miles west of the town of Emporia, near the Cottonwood River, when I come across a little road that looks like it might need investigating, a road I just know, at a glance, will peter out somewhere in gravel and dirt next to an old wooden farm shack and a dead tractor, or at the edge of a yard where a fat, gun-shy dog sits dreaming on a broken porch, next to a plot of jimsonweed and pumpkins. This is Osage country, the gnarled, bitter fruits of the Osage orange scattered along the banks of the rivers and gullies like live green rubble in the one section of Kansas that isn't pancake flat, right at the edge of the Flint Hills; and even if the old prairie is gone, a few oases of bluegrass remain, not blue now, but rust-red and coppery and golden in the autumn light, a few last tatters of the real Midwest preserved by government decree to remind this casual visitor of what made this land so magical in our great-great-grandfathers' time.

So I make a detour (a detour within a detour, really) and turn off the highway, knowing I'll see nobody for miles, and glad of the fact, wanting to imagine myself alone in the world for a while, travelling in splendid isolation, the singular luxury that the Midwest still afforded in those days. There's nothing remarkable about this road, and it leads to what is usually called nowhere, which is why the rest of my day is so pleasant. I don't want local colour; I don't want the picturesque. I do not, under any circumstances, want anything recognisable as history. I want the here and now, the ordinary quotidian, the subtle beauty of the unremarkable. As I drive, I see no real landmarks, other than the occasional cottonwood, nestled into a gully, turning water into shade, and the odd stretch of fence (wood, not wire) around what looks like a derelict farm, but may well be somebody's entire life.

So I drive on that little road a while, then I turn back, pretty much satisfied. To a casual visitor, this is nowhere, but to me, for that one day at least, it's one of those magical places where nothing happens. Which is maybe why, when I return a few weeks later, on the drive back, I can't find it: no cottonwoods, no dark farm, not even the turning at which I first entered this hinterland. I drive for miles and I watch for it all the way, but I never see it. It was an illusion, a phantom, the Kansas version of Brigadoon. Later still, when I get back to the place where I am staying and take out the map, I can't find anything that corresponds with the road I had driven on that now already mythical afternoon. Mythical – well, for me, at least, it was, and is: a chapter in the story of my real self that has no particular significance anywhere else. Not even a chapter, really, but a fleeting idea, an image, a metaphor.

When we were children and somebody would talk to us about the next world, it always came over as mystical or religious, a stray notion from a province of wishful thinking normally inhabited by children and the simple-minded, as opposed to the real, factual, less deceived world of grown-ups and rationalists. Well, I'm not the type for that kind of thing. Our Scholar-Murderer would probably have fun debating terms like *mystical* and *religious* and *rational*, but to me the only world is here, now, but we lose sight of it every day, we miss it, we see what we expect to see and we think as we're expected to think. All the time, growing up, I wanted to uncover that missed world – that's why I took up science – and, by extension, the missed self who sees and imagines and is fully alive outside the bounds of the usual expectations, not by some rational process (or not as the term is usually understood) but by a kind of radical illumination, a re-attunement to the continuum of objects and weather and other lives that we inhabit. We might say, if we could strip away the accretions of dogma and prejudice that have attached to the gospels over centuries, that Jesus' argument in the gospels – the Kingdom of Heaven is at hand – is scientifically rather sound. All he was demanding of his listeners was that they would see the world as it really is. Yet it makes as much sense to call this a scientific problem as it does to call it religious, for this discipline of the imagination is the central human concern and, without it, there can be no real knowledge. Without that knowledge, we are lost, in a world we do not understand but try vainly to control; without it, we are exactly where the powers-that-be want us: malleable, predictable, and slavishly in thrall to the hydra-headed monsters of entertainment and consumption. Without it, we are passively, if rather sullenly guided through life by road maps prepared for us, not by others *per se*, but by a machinery of hellish otherness in which we, as persons, are hopelessly entangled.'

I stopped talking. He was watching me, a little surprised, but clearly pleased. 'Go on,' he said.

I shook my head. 'That's about it,' I said. 'What I really wanted to say is that I know, now, that the way to enter the life to come is to stumble upon it, on those rare occasions when I am not distracted by the usual business of existing: work, worry, being among others, the way I did that day, outside Emporia, Kansas. I can pick out moments, lasting from a few seconds at a time to an hour, to a whole afternoon or night, when I have entered into that world and, though there is no narrative attached to such incidents that allows for a retelling, I find myself returning, again and again, to memories that I cannot share with others, or even pin down fully for myself.'

Ben nodded. 'I know what you mean,' he said.

He did, too. But there was something else – something true – that I wanted to tell him now, only I couldn't be sure he would believe it. 'Some time after that drive in the Flint Hills, on another highway, a thousand miles from Kansas, I came across the same turning, the same country road, the same glimmers of cottonwood seed drifting across the fields. I noticed it immediately and, turning off the main road, I drove for twenty miles or so till the track fizzled out in a sandy wash, a line of willows, a silence broken now and then by the call of a red-winged blackbird, crouched among the reeds. It was a warm, egg-blue and straw-coloured afternoon, and I was nowhere in particular; but that's the thing about the life to come: it turns up in the most unlikely places, when you least expect it.'

He nodded, and smiled happily. 'Thank you,' he said. 'That's a good story.'

'It's not much of –'

He raised a finger to his lips. 'Sh,' he said. 'Here, we treat every story as a gift. It's the best test we have and…'

'Test of what?'

'Whether the teller is true or not.'

'I'd hardly lie about a cross-country trip, twenty years ago,' I said.

He smiled. 'More than that now,' he said. 'Seventy years. More.' He shook his head. 'Time, eh?' he said.

AUTOBIOGRAPHY OF
JOHN THE GARDENER

*Unfinished, found in a desk at Havergey House, 2050:
Entry for autumn 2036 (?)*

Last of the rain for a while, time to renew the big bonfire at the far corner of the paddock, one of my favourite jobs. Some years, it burns for days in the autumn time. I had to cut down two trees, a flowering apple and a fine plum, with beautiful, golden yellow fruits, after the last storm, so there is plenty to burn. I was there when the apple came down, it just fractured in the wind, then turned in on itself and fell – very strange, like a dancer losing her balance – a scatter of tiny new crab apples bouncing across the cold frame. Now the first of the boughs has been offered to the flames, the damp wood crackling and spitting in the gathering flames, the wet boughs scabbed with moss and lichen.

It was a bad end to the summer. I don't know how it happened, but something came in on the wind, a thick powder almost like pollen, and settled on the fish pond. I saw it happen, but I couldn't do anything – standing at the edge of the pond, holding a rag to my nose, I didn't know what it was, but I wasn't surprised when, by daybreak next morning, every single fish in the pond was dead, bodies risen to the surface in sad islands of greying flesh, the water curdled with rot, the stench of it thick in my nose and eyes as I leant from the Japanese bridge, gathering samples. Pointless, of course – and if he had been here, the old man would have told me so. He would have been right, too – and anyway, even if I had worked out what that strange powder drifting in on the air had been, I still wouldn't have known where it came from, or worse still, whether there would be more of it.

*

I have kept the clocks running all through Havergey House, and that's quite a task, when there is so much else to do. But then, I have always loved the minor, everyday jobs, the daily round of maintenance, of cleaning and oiling and calibrating, the weekly routines and the seasonal work – all of it. I still rake the leaves and windfalls in the orchard and every autumn I have a great bonfire, like the fires of old, to clear away the dead boughs and whatever else has been damaged by the late summer storms. Sometimes I wonder how much longer this will continue, and what the place will look like when I am gone – and at times I also consider why I am the last, whether I was chosen for a reason to keep the estate in good condition for the sake of – what? Something to come? Someone? I have a notion there are people on the mainland still: I saw lights on the far shore a few months back, after everything had been dark for a long time, and I picked up odd sounds on the radio for a while, though that's all gone now. Still, who knows if people might not come here some day? If they do, I hope they make better use of Havergey than Hugh Follansbee did.

Hugh Follansbee. It would always intrigue me, the way he behaved. The way he seemed to accept so naturally that he was the centre of the world. I would ask myself how anyone could acquire that sense of entitlement. Was it inborn? No – I am sure every newborn child, no matter what their blood, has it in them to be decent, even humble. It's only when someone is educated to think he is superior, educated from the moment of birth that

[AROUND FIVE LINES HERE ILLEGIBLE]

to be told all the time: You are a Follansbee, you are the firstborn, one day all of this will be yours. All of Havergey, people included. Which was pretty much true. They didn't come up with the word 'tied' for nothing – and it didn't just refer to cottages, it was a matter of livelihood, reputation, and loyalty, however misplaced. I'm ashamed to say I felt it myself, growing up. When 'our' new iris and rhododendron cultivars won prizes at some big London flower show – oh, how I longed to go to Chelsea, just to see it all first-hand – I felt a justified pride, because the man who had made those hybrids was my father. Yes, I felt proud; until I noticed that this father of mine, John Graham, was never mentioned in the magazine articles and gardening programmes. Hugh Follansbee was. His lovely wife was and two of the best rhododendrons were named for her. But not John Graham.

When I complained about that, my father would laugh. 'That's how it always goes,' he would say. 'But it doesn't matter, if everyone gets what he wants in the end.'

'But it does matter,' I would say. 'Why should he get – '

'Hush, son,' he would say then, his face softening. 'We're not in this for the glory. We are gardeners. We serve the garden. Not the master, not the estate, but the garden. That's our only privilege, but it's a wonderful gift.'

'But the garden belongs – '

'The garden belongs to nobody.' He shook his head with a glad finality. 'Ownership of the land – that's an illusion. The earth cannot belong to us, or to Hugh Follansbee, but we, at least, can belong to the earth. We have that – but poor old Hugh Follansbee doesn't. We have enough to eat and drink, we have decent shelter and we have the garden. If Hugh Follansbee tried to take any of that away from us, I would open his head with a mattock and bury him the West Wood.' He smiled then, his eyes twinkling at the thought – and I knew he would have done just that, had the occasion called for it. 'For now, though, everyone has what he needs and, if some of it is an illusion, that isn't our problem.'

Well, that was all very well for him. He got what he wanted out of life, partly because he wanted so little, but some of us were less fortunate under Hugh Follansbee's tyranny. He wasn't a consistent dictator, perhaps, but he was ruthless, and I think, if I had only

*

At this point, the autobiography suddenly breaks off and, though it is possible that John Graham continued to write it in some other form – maybe in another notebook that is now lost – it seems unlikely. He had been writing for a reason, trying to work something out and now, it seems, he had found something that invalidated any hope he'd had of seeing a pattern, an order, a meaning in the story he had been trying to tell. He'd been hoping to take an ordinary life that didn't seem complete enough, or maybe rich enough to him, and give it some extra dimension, some fuller shape, by making it a story. But it hadn't worked. Now, alone on the estate, his old enemy gone, his first love lost, he didn't know any more what was true and what wasn't. All he knew was that it was over. He was alone now – and there were other things to think about.

ISLAND OF HAVERGEY

An Excursion around the Island,
including Havergey House and its Environs,

by 'Chloë'

Something was wrong. I had been trying for days, now, to put a story together and I had almost all the pieces of the puzzle, but there were still so many unknowns about how they linked together, I might as well have had nothing at all. Clearly, Yvonne had betrayed Hugh with her cousin Felix and, clearly, Max had played some part in helping to cover up the affair. I knew that Chloë was Felix's daughter, not Hugh's – and yet, it seems, Hugh suspected nothing until, suddenly, he discovered the truth, possibly because Chloë told him, though I could not be sure of this, and sent Yvonne and her daughter to Spain. I had no idea why they had gone to Spain – family, perhaps? If so, where was Felix when they got there? He would have been in England some time around then, for Max says that he and the mystery woman, Tiziana, had been arrested at that time. What happened to the rest of the anarchist cell was still a mystery. Why was Felix in England with Tiziana? Were they plotting something? Was she his lover now? In some of the photographs, there had been something between them. A closeness. A complicity. I was beginning to entertain bad thoughts about cousin Felix.

So – when Hugh sends Chloë away, John thinks it is on his account. But he writes his autobiography, such as it is, years later, when all the other players in this little tragedy are dead. Was I meant to believe that, when John had the whole estate to himself, the Gardener never once looked at Max's papers? His letter to Paola? His notebooks? Examining all the evidence, I can only conclude that he did not – and a picture was forming in my mind, an image of John as an honourable man, a discreet friend, a romantic figure who never really stood a chance among these people. He was an innocent, and something of a fool when it came to Chloë (who seems to have forgotten him, pretty well, after only a short time away) but he was a good person. The very thought of prying into Max's affairs would have horrified him. Which, presumably, means that he never found out the truth about Chloë's disappearance. Presumably – but it was like reading a novel with several pages missing. Not only did I not have all the necessary facts, I didn't know how all the people felt about one another. What did Yvonne feel about Hugh, for example? Or about Felix? And what kind of person was *she*? Was Hugh really as bad as everybody seemed to think he was? In a good novel, or a film, he would have had a human side, some redeeming feature. That's the rule in fiction: nobody is all bad. Here, though, wherever he appears, he is a petty tyrant, despised by all and, finally, the kind of person who would sink so low as to condemn two people he probably knew were nothing more than dilettante revolutionists, to prison, certain torture and an early death.

But there was more to this story, I thought. Something was missing. Some clue, some passing remark, some term of endearment or nickname or half-told memory that I hadn't found yet. I wandered the practice room, thinking it all through; I stood at the window, staring out at the snow. This story, in the absence of anything else to think about – and, I suppose, now, because I didn't want to think about the past, about what happened to the people I had known, people like Abigail, say – this story was starting to obsess me. But how could I find the answer? Where was the missing clue? All I could do was read what was left of The Archive. There was nothing else to do.

*

I found Chloë's 'Excursion' in a large manila envelope covered with stamps, and addressed simply to Max Jedermann, Havergey. In the top margin of the first page, above the title, she had written:

Darling Nuncle, what do you think? It's not finished yet, but I thought it might make a good piece to start my new career. Do you think The Lady *would take it? Or maybe* Scottish Field*?*

Directly below, Max had written: *OK. But it needs more flow, Chlo…* And here the piece, such as it is, begins.

*

VIII

To step off the boat at the island of Havergey is to come to a place that is, as the cliché goes, steeped in history, but it is not the history we learned in school. All those tedious kings and bishops and popes, all the treaties and royal marriages and battles, as if these were the only events that mattered, and the real people, the folk, the balladeers and book illuminators, the farriers and reddlemen, the women forced into nunneries and the women forced into marriage, the tavern singers and the gardeners, all forgotten, or ignored. But none of this seems to matter on Havergey. Here, history is concealed in the land, in old burial sites and holy trees that, if you didn't know what you were looking for, you wouldn't know were there. People have always lived on Havergey, but somehow they managed to avoid the rule of kings and lords and other tyrants for centuries – right up until the coming of the Follansbees, around two hundred years ago. Until then, the history of Havergey has more to do with the natural world, with what you might call natural history, than the human – and where the human intrudes, it feels like something from an Arthurian romance, which isn't officially history, I know, but then how do we really live? Do we dwell in officialdom or legend?

[Here, Max has scribbled into the margin: *stick to the point* – which is a bit rich, coming from him.]

Dear old Arthur, who might have been king, but he knew his main ability was to recognise the abilities of others. How many kings had that much humility? Frederick the Great, maybe. Most monarchs turn out mediocre, it seems. Lords and such, too – though I'd like to know more about some of them before I rush to judgement. For instance, William the Silent sounds promising, but I'm scared to look him up in case he ends up being a disappointment too.

OK, fresh start. I'm just warming up here.

The fact is that, when we study history as if all that mattered was power and property, then we are bound to believe that power and property are all that matter. Which they do – but that's because… Well, it's a vicious circle, isn't it? I think

[Here, an asterisk appears and a new tone emerges, as if she is attempting to channel a classic novel she has recently consumed, or at least, dipped into.]

The rich man who acquires an estate likes to think of himself as its master, its informing genius and guiding hand when, in fact the opposite is much more likely: the less he interferes, the more the land prospers, for the getting of money and the getting of wisdom seldom come together in one man's life. If a man were wise, he would hardly seek to acquire property to excess; if he were just, he would not feast while others starved; if he were that rarest of creatures, a gentleman, he would give credit where it was due and not pretend to others, or to himself, that his good luck was some kind of accomplishment. For several generations, however, the men who owned Havergey fooled themselves into thinking that they were the guardians of this place, the presiding spirits whose duty it was to oversee the work done by others and so shape the place to their own vision. In truth, they were tyrants, nothing more. The incumbent landowner may pretend to treasure the gardens and meadows as a steward does, but for him, the land, like his various animal possessions, his dogs and horses and such, is simply an extension – and an illustration – of his superior character.

The older gardener here, John Graham, has a saying – he

says it in the Gaelic, but if you ask him to, he will grudgingly translate the phrase as *his nature breaks out on him*. It means, as I understand it, that a man can pretend all he likes to be decent, or just, or even noble, but in a crisis, especially where it comes to property or status, he shows his true colours. His nature breaks out on him – it sounds like some awful disease, a pox out of nowhere, running wild on his skin, and scabbing his face. Sometimes, I picture the island in its perfect state: not as Hugh Follansbee and his ancestors made it, but as it could have been, had we been absent. We all read about Chernobyl with Max – young John, the old gardener's son, was fascinated by it. How in no more than twenty years the land had gone back to how it was before people came there, great meadows of wild grasses, huge herds of deer, wolves in the trees, their eyes like lit candles in the shadows. Imagine the whole world like that, swarming, teeming with animals and birds and fishes. Not so long ago – less than two hundred years, a mere blip in the annals of this land – Havergey would have been like that.

Then came Thomas Edison Follansbee, followed by his son, Hugh, men who never tired of proclaiming the need for 'order' – which, in the garden, meant straight lines in the lawns, crisp perfect edges around the herbaceous borders, raked gravel, all that sense of avenue and vista and pleached hedge that, all very well in its place, becomes absurd in a garden like this. Yet the worst thing (certainly the thing the gardeners disliked most) was the abundance of clipped and manicured grass around Havergey House: the front lawn, the back lawn, the croquet lawn, the tennis lawn that nobody ever used, the secret lawn (hidden away in an angle by the library), the list goes on – every one had to be just so. Old Thomas, by all accounts, was a 'real stickler' for a tidy lawn. During his years as master of Havergey, all the grassed areas were perfect (that is, perfectly dull) from the baize-coloured nap of the croquet lawn on the south side of the Scholar's Wing, to the wide swathe of green pasture that ran from the Orangery to the ha-ha. When Hugh inherited, he carried on what he called *the Havergey tradition* – and he did it with a vengeance.

When I was a little girl, I used to learn poems by heart. The first I got to know was what might have been the last poem Edward Thomas wrote, 'Out in the dark'. I could do Mercutio's Queen Mab speech from *Romeo and Juliet*, too, and there was one long one I really liked that I can't recall in its entirety now, about a painter who falls in love with a creature of his own imagining, a creature 'half-girl; half-frost'. I liked that. But my favourite poem of all was Coleridge's nightingale poem. That was pretty long too, but I had it all by heart and I still remember it.

> And I know a grove
> Of large extent, hard by a castle huge,
> Which the great lord inhabits not; and so
> This grove is wild with tangling underwood,
> And the trim walks are broken up, and grass,
> Thin grass and king-cups grow within the paths.
> But never elsewhere in one place I knew
> So many nightingales; and far and near,
> In wood and thicket, over the wide grove,
> They answer and provoke each other's song,
> With skirmish and capricious passagings,

And murmurs musical and swift jug jug,
And one low piping sound more sweet than all
Stirring the air with such a harmony,
That should you close your eyes, you might almost
Forget it was not day!

I liked that too. How the land prospers, when the great lord is gone. Now that they are no longer bounded by his possession, the meadows seem limitless; the woods beyond have become a bright hypothesis, like the middle distance in a mediaeval painting. And the nightingales are everywhere. Just because the lord is gone, and nature has been allowed to take its course.

Letting nature take its course. We talk about that often, in Hugh Follansbee's manicured domain. It is our central dream. Our idea of heaven.

★

At this point, several lines have been deleted, or rather, obliterated by repeated scorings so that the letters are no longer legible. In the margin Chloë has written: *All right, it's a mess. All I really want to say is the thing about history. How it has to be a history of everyone, and the land.*

– and directly below, Max has written: *If at first you don't succeed, try coming at it from a different direction.*

The rest of the page is blank, and what follows is a series of typed pages, with titles and notes, though it's far from cohesive and most of it feels like a draft at something Chloë may well have been incapable of producing, at her age. At the head of the next page, she has typed:

HAVERGEY HOUSE

As far as I know, nobody at Havergey is genuinely religious.
Well, maybe Nuncle is. As for me, I don't mind ideas like
God (that's just another word for nature, so far as I can see),
and some religious art is genuinely moving, but what I can't
stomach is the notion of life after death. I think I would
throw away everything that is interesting about religion, just
to be rid of the idea of heaven. Or, if it could not be avoided,
I'd take my afterlife in the ornamental margins of the 1350
St Denis Missal, a reasonable copy of which is preserved in
Havergey Chapel. (Yes, Hugh Follansbee has a chapel. For
some reason, he thinks every medium-sized country house
should have one.) In the margins of the St Denis Missal,
birds and butterflies flit through the summer air (no material
fabric suggests the summer air so well as the parchment of
that period), long vines of acanthus leaves proliferate out of
the text, winding into the white space in elaborate designs;
the suggestion, overall, is of warmth and, at the same time,
freshness: a summer's morning, say, before the sun reaches its
zenith, when the smell of the dew, or a breath of the sea wind
lingers on the air.

John the Gardener says he believes there is a life after death,
but that it isn't personal. How he pictures it is, there will be an
ending, a long passage through decay and regeneration and,
finally (though there would, of course, be no sense of time to
any of this) an emergence in which who knows what would
remain of what had gone before. John has long talks with
Nuncle about religious and philosophical stuff, like rebirth,
and metempsychosis, and I do believe part of him accepts the
possibility of some kind of reincarnation, but he is a gardener,

and I think he would immediately have seen the irony in the story: that, having lost what he loved, he would be born again as something else, with no memory of that previous life – and why would anybody want to come back, if not to return to what they loved? Nuncle reminds him that this is an example of attachment – and he points out that dying and returning would absolve him of any attachment to specific individuals and instances, so that he might come to love all of creation, but John doesn't accept that – or rather, he can't shake off the hope that, somewhere, beyond the fact of persons, he would re-encounter the handful of people and animals and places he has loved so fiercely – and yet, so very quietly – during his time as John the Gardener. And I don't judge him for that – after all, who would not want to meet their loved ones in some future life, no matter how slender a proposition it might seem? Nuncle, on the other hand, a man steeped in Eastern philosophy, is always puzzled by this. Can John not see that a soul might be reborn many times, and that in each life, it would form attachments that seemed more precious than anything else it could imagine – and in fact, according to his philosophy, it is the philosophical elegance of the idea of reincarnation that those many rebirths would allow each soul to love the whole of creation in the same way as it had loved those special instances.

[HERE THE TEXT BREAKS OFF AGAIN, AND IS FOLLOWED BY A NEW HEADING.]

HAVERGEY VILLAGE

If it is not driven by development (that is, by money), a village emerges in response to its physical surroundings

– and the weather, of course. At one time, Havergey was such a village, but it has to be said that the reign of the Follansbees compromised that spontaneous process. Luckily, not as much as Brother Hugh intended, for which I thank the spirits of this place – and London, of course, where the pickings are easy and far from slim, or easy, at least for a man of Brother Hugh's calibre. We also thank the earth spirits for Thomas Edison Follansbee's father, Ashworth Follansbee, crafty old bugger that he was. Somehow he foresaw Hugh's coming, and arranged things so that any heir, no matter how obnoxious, would have to respect the essential virtues of Havergey Village. Cottages were to be maintained to a high standard, and rents fixed (Hugh managed to get round some of that, with his merry band of quick brown lawyers); there would always be a well-stocked library, with librarian, on the island; the harbour would only be used for fishing boats below a certain size. There would be no ferry port; anyone who wanted to get to the mainland would have to negotiate with the pilot of the mail boat, which came in twice a week, on Mondays and Thursdays. At every turn, he closed off every scheme someone like Hugh might come up with – some of them not even anticipated by most folk back then. In my mind's eye, I see him, walking around the harbour and out across the meadows, stopping to talk to one of his tenant farmers – he had no factor, which was rare in those days, when every estate was overseen by just such a person, loathed by all, though high in his own estimation – then rambling out to the furthest corners of the island, looking for ways in which the greedy and the small-minded might try to turn the good land to a quick profit. The one thing he didn't anticipate was the wind turbine – but I shall talk of that later.

It could be argued, then, that old Ashworth Follansbee was something of a utopian in his day. And by that token, it could also be argued that the real Havergey – the Havergey he wanted to set in motion, unimpeded, to find its way in the world, as it were – is still only a place in the mind, one man's speculation, like More's *Utopia*, or in William Morris' more satisfying *News from Nowhere* – and, like these and other speculations, it is a place that celebrates possibilities, rather than limits.

In short, this village continues to dwell in Possibility, a fairer House than Prose (as Emily Dickinson put it) – and all these years after Ashworth died, after the predation of Hugh and his father, it has not given up on possibility. If there is one word in the English language I dislike (and it is a rare thing for me to dislike a word as such) it is *dystopian* – a word that shouts of self rather than world, of cleverness rather than intelligence, and it is helpful now and then to remind ourselves that the opposite of intelligence is not stupidity, but this uniquely smug vice. Few creatures seem as surplus to evolutionary requirements as the clever ones. *Clever* is the word used on Havergey to describe intricately formal poetry that does not descend into the everyday world the rest of us inhabit by attempting to express, however obliquely, something that might nourish the listener's beleaguered spirits. *Clever* is irony-as-a-veil and allusion for its own sake (even while I confine these remarks to poetry, which, being portable, is the art form most favoured by Havergey folk, it is clear that everything a work of art includes, no matter how surprising, must seem *called-for*).

However, as the old novelists used to say, I digress. I was discussing my distaste for the word dystopian – though to express this both fully and succinctly (the first I might attempt alone, the second I feel altogether unfurnished to tackle, as this wordy aside perfectly demonstrates) I could do no better than call upon the father of the English novel himself, Samuel Richardson, who, in *Clarissa, or, the History of a Young Lady*, declares that: 'Hope is the cordial that keeps life from stagnating.' This is not to say that diagnostic analysis of social conditions and problems should not inform a novel; indeed, the best utopian novels propose, at the very least, an implicit critique of their author's social milieu, laws and customs.

(Another digression, though hopefully more pertinent: the first time the word dystopian goes down in recorded usage is when J.S. Mill invokes it, in March 1868, to speak, not of a fictional situation, but of *catastrophic real life conditions* caused by the British government's policies in Ireland. In a long and spirited speech, he derides the Conservative government of the day thus: 'I may be permitted, as one who, in common with many of my betters, has been subjected to the charge of being Utopian, to congratulate the Government on having joined that goodly company. It is, perhaps, too complimentary to call them Utopians, they ought rather to be called dystopians, or cacotopians. What is commonly called Utopian is something too good to be practicable; but what they appear to favour is too bad to be practicable.'

It is one thing to invoke the dystopian paradigm in criticising actual events, whether in Parliament or in a piece of fiction, but to conjure it up in a *speculative* work is – unless it is hugely comical – as pointless a luxury as can be imagined. We already know, following Emerson, that every actual state is corrupt. As soon as an edifice is built, as soon as a frontier is opened, as soon as a law has been made, the woodworm begins to hatch, the speculators arrive and the lawyers commence searching for loopholes. To most dystopian works, I want to reply: Tell me something I don't know, while almost any utopian novel, however naïve in places, sets me to thinking. So, while I would maintain that *my* Havergey is as real a place as any that could be found on a current map, I would contend that it is also a speculation that might provoke some new thoughts on what is understood by notions like justice and community – concepts that, in recent years, have been subjected to an astonishing level of distortion and abuse by government, Big Business and the unending procession of local entrepreneurs and politicians (people who used to be referred to as 'bounders') that turns up wherever there is something good to betray, something fine to 'develop' or any loophole in policy that allows them to practice their ugly trade.

[HERE SHE BREAKS OFF AGAIN. THE NEXT PAGE, HOWEVER, IS EVEN MORE DISORGANISED.]

THE SCHOOLHOUSE

– sits at the centre of the village, adjacent to The Green, by Ashworth Follansbee's decree. In his day, it was a pleasant place, run by a kindly but strict spinster (his term, not mine) who instructed the children in 'the basics', including arithmetic, writing in a clean hand, a little science, and a little more scripture. More recently, it has seemed less kindly, and the teacher somewhat less fastidious. Which only raises the hypothetical question that: if an education system was no longer tailored to the needs of some hypothetical future employer (as Hugh's school is) and if we could teach our children anything at all, what would we do? The first question one might ask is whether to have school at all, but I think a schoolhouse of some sort should exist, as long as attendance remains optional. That way, people would be more likely to participate fully. Each day, the class would decide whether they would meet the next day, or the day after that and, when that was agreed, they would set a time convenient to all. If a child chose to, he or she could skip classes on any particular day, though if they planned to be away for more than one day, they would inform the teacher of this, as a courtesy. Yet, even though this might be permitted, I don't think it would happen often. In fact, I think the children would enjoy school so much, they would devise curriculum items of their own design – and

[HERE, ONCE AGAIN, SHE MOVES ON, EVER MORE IMPATIENT.]

THE WALLED GARDEN

Old John Graham bred several new cultivars of iris, rhododendron and lily, but he wasn't permitted to name them. Hugh Follansbee took that privilege to himself. Nuncle says, to name something is an act of goodwill, but it is also a privilege –

★

And here, all at once, the typescript ends, or rather, stops. In the space directly below these last lines, Max has written:

Don't worry. There's plenty of promising stuff here. The thing you have to decide is, what do you really want to write about? Is it Havergey, or history, or the afterlife. Or is it something

else entirely? If you can work that out, you have good material here for starting over.

The rest of the page is blank, however. By the time Nuncle wrote these encouraging words, Chloë may very well have been dead. We'll never know, but the fact that he didn't send the notes back to her suggests that this is the most likely scenario.

QUARANTINE

When he brought supper that evening, Ben was not alone. His companion was a tall, grey-haired woman of around fifty, a woman who looked, to me, like she might once have been a yoga teacher, or maybe a gymnast. I had never met anyone who seemed to live so perfectly in her own body; there was a gravity about her, an elegance, that I felt sure she must have been born with – and anything she did later had only brought this natural gift to perfection. Around her, Ben seemed a little – I don't know. Not deferential, exactly, and there was nothing awkward about the way he behaved. It was just that he seemed to regard this woman as somehow different from other people, a person who had been touched by something otherworldly.

'Angharad asked to meet you,' he said.

The woman nodded. 'Ben told me you've come from the past,' she said, as if this was the most natural thing in the world.

'Yes,' I said. I tried to think of something more to say, but I couldn't.

'Ben also thinks you're ready to join us,' she said. 'Do you think that's true?'

'I don't know,' I said. 'As I understand it, I have to stay here in case –'

She raised her hand and, without intending to, I stopped talking. 'When you are ready, you will know,' she said. 'Until then, you have to stay in Quarantine. But that's the only reason you have to stay.'

'So, I don't have some kind of infectious disease?'

She shook her head. 'Not my job to say,' she said. 'Though I doubt it. Apart from being a man who hasn't slept well in – what? fifteen years? – you're as fit as can be expected.' She looked around, then moved over to the table and sat down. This seemed to be a sign for Ben to begin his usual routine of unpacking the food for our meal.

'Ben said you came here to study the weather,' Angharad said. 'He says you weren't looking for – anything else.'

'I didn't know what I'd find,' I said. And though that was true, it didn't *sound* true and I felt strangely guilty, as if I had caught myself telling a deliberate lie.

'Well, what you found was – this place. Havergey. And tomorrow, or the day after, or... *soon*, you get to see it for yourself, instead of just hearing about it. Soon you will meet the others and you will have the opportunity to see what we are trying to do here with your own eyes. So I want to tell you something. Just so you know.'

I nodded. 'I understand,' I said.

She frowned. 'I haven't said anything yet.'

'I know,' I said. 'It's just – I think I know what you want to say.'

She smiled. 'Ah,' she said. 'Well, then. Go ahead.'

'There's no such place as Utopia.'

She shook her head.

'No?'

'Not wrong,' she said. 'But not right either. There is no such place as Utopia, it's not a state, just as happiness is not a state. But they happen, nevertheless.' She smiled, but it seemed to me that she was uncertain – and what occurred to me now was something I should have guessed as soon as I met her. It had been staring me in the face and I hadn't put it all together right away, but now I saw that Ben had been there to tell me stories, to introduce me to the idea of Havergey, but he wasn't there to decide anything. Angharad may well have been another Watcher, and she was probably a very good one, but she was something else too. Maybe the people here didn't call it by the name I was giving it in my own mind, but at that moment I knew that, really, when the situation called for such things, Angharad was a judge. 'So,' she said. 'Ben has told you pretty much all you need to know about what you'll find when – if – you pass through that door –'

'Is there any other option?' I said, surprising myself. I had been careful, all this time, not to presume.

Angharad laughed. 'There are always options,' she said. 'We must think of the community first. You may be part of that community, but I don't know, yet, if that's the case.' She studied my face for a moment, then she looked away. Out in the dark, over the snow, a faint blue gloaming hung over the meadow. 'Well,' she said, finally. 'One thing is certain.' She turned back to face me. 'Now that you know what you know, we can't send you back to where you came from.' She smiled.

IX

'Even if we did know how.'

'I guess not.'

'So: what do you think about that?'

'What do you mean?'

'Well, all those people,' she said. 'The fact that everyone you know…' She stood up and walked over to the great window, while Ben silently put the food bowls out on the table. 'I sometimes wonder, in my idler moments, if anything lingers of them. If they leave anything behind. Wisps of love and desire and grief for what they missed, clinging to the earth like…' She put her hand against the dark glass. I couldn't see her face, just a ghostly reflection in the window. 'They would have loved. They would have had children. How did it feel, to die, and not be able to explain to your children that it didn't matter? Or rather, that it wouldn't matter if those children could live their own lives – full lives, lives rich in memory and forgetting…' She turned back to look at me. 'What do you think about that?'

I shook my head. 'I never thought about it that way,' I said.

'You never had children,' she said.

'No.'

'But you must have loved –'

'I had my work,' I said. 'And there was music. If you asked me to say what I loved most, back then, I'd have to say, if I could only choose one thing to cherish, it would be a piece by Miles Davis. *Nuit Sur Les Champs-Élysées.*'

'I don't know what that is,' she said. 'And it seems to me that you're being evasive.'

'Well,' I said. 'It doesn't matter what I think, does it?'

She seemed genuinely surprised by this. 'Oh no,' she said.

'That's completely upside down. Completely upside down.'
She shook her head. 'It doesn't matter to me or to you
what *other people* think. It matters what they *feel*, but that's
something else. What *you* think is crucial. Always.'

'For whom?'

'For you, first,' she said. 'But also for everyone – *everything*
– around you. In a small, almost forensic and yet significant
way, what you think is everything.'

'I don't understand.'

'We make all this together. Moment by moment. It's real,
but it's improvised. For us, Utopia is neither here nor there.
What matters is that Havergey is a garden. What matters
most to us, now, and to you, is whether or not you want to
think as a gardener.'

'Ah,' I said. Suddenly I understood why they valued John
the Gardener's book so highly. The Scholar had laid out the
principles, a basic, if somewhat desultory philosophy for their
Creation Myth, but John's rambling autobiography had laid
the basis for their practice. All those commonplaces – all the
quotes from Spinoza and William Morris and Lao Tse – had
to be balanced by the astrantia and the ox-eye daisies growing
wild through the long grasses on the great lawn, years after
they had been banished forever from the estate.

Angharad nodded. 'You know,' she said. 'There was a man,
back in your era.' She considered a moment. 'He said that
the catastrophe that threatens a degrading society is not its
punishment, but its remedy.'

I laughed. 'He wouldn't have said that, if he'd known
what was coming,' I said.

She laughed. 'On the contrary,' she said. 'He saw what was

coming all too well. *That*'s why he said it.'

I nodded. Of course, she was right. More people had known what was coming than admitted as much, and a fair few of them thought that catastrophe was the only remedy we had left. A thousand Chernobyls. Maybe I was one of those people, in my darkest moments, at least. Then I would sit down, alone in my apartment, and put the soundtrack to *Ascenseur pour l'échafaud* on the machine and I would picture Jeanne Moreau wandering the streets of Paris, wondering where her lover has gone, and I would do my best to believe otherwise. 'All right,' I said. 'I have one request.'

Angharad looked grave. I didn't know what she was expecting, but her face darkened and set then, as if she was afraid I would refuse the only gift she had to offer.

'My notes,' I said. 'I told my colleagues I would at least try to get them back –'

'You can't do that,' she said. 'You know it's not possible.'

'But I have to try.'

At that, her face relaxed, the darkness and doubt replaced by sadness for my predicament. 'You can try,' she said. 'But see Havergey first. Get to know us. Then you can go back to your...' She searched for an appropriate word for Tardis B, then gave up. 'There are no walls here. No fences. You can go back to your machine at any time. If it's a fine day, I'll walk out there with you myself. Just don't tell them you've found...'

'Utopia?'

She laughed softly. 'Whatever you do,' she said. 'Don't tell them that.'

By now, Ben had finished his tasks – though clearly, he had been taking his time so Angharad could say what she had to say. 'Supper's ready,' he said.

I glanced back at the window. Out on the meadow, the moon had suddenly come out, and it was very bright. A moment before, the land had been dark. I paused a moment, taking it all in – the moon, the snowy meadow, the trees – then I sat down and we began to eat, in silence now, as if there was nothing more to be said until some change, some decision, had been made.

THE WIND TURBINE

When Ben had brought Angharad to the quarantine house, I'd thought I was done reading Chloë's 'excursion', but when I went back to put the manuscript away, I found another typed sheet in the envelope that I must have missed – and it seemed fitting, somehow, that I should go back then to that child's-eye view of a Utopia she never got to see. When I pulled out the extra sheet of paper, however, I saw that it contained nothing but a heading, and a single sentence. The heading said: Hugh Follansbee's Wind Turbine and, below it, scrawled in Chloë's spidery handwriting, the words: *Oh, the stupidity of it all*.

And that was all. No further comment, either from Chloë, or from Max. I smiled. I understood exactly what she meant, but for me, it seemed like just yesterday (and it was, in a way) that we were erecting these absurd machines (though every self-respecting engineer, energy expert, physicist, ornithologist and student of peatland ecology – in fact, pretty well anybody qualified to have an opinion, had pointed out how utterly pointless and destructive those machines were). I remembered all this, and I remembered James Lovelock, a man I found brilliant and exasperating in almost equal measure, giving evidence to some committee, back around 2013, on the folly of relying on wind energy to 'keep the lights on' (that's what people always said, which was revealing in itself: it had long been time to turn a few of the lights off). On that day, Lovelock said: 'I am an environmentalist and founder member of the Greens but I bow my head in shame at the thought that our original good intentions should have been so misunderstood and misapplied. We never intended a fundamentalist Green movement that rejected all energy sources other than renewable, nor did we expect the Greens to cast aside our priceless ecological heritage because of their failure to understand that the needs of the Earth are not separable from human needs. We need to take care that the spinning windmills do not become like the statues on Easter Island, monuments of a failed civilisation.' Well, our civilisation had failed, all right, and sooner than any of us had expected – and I was glad, in a way, that I hadn't been there to see it. Happier still, that I had never had children. Though that was foolish too, because my children might have been among those who swam, or rowed, or rafted the sound and came here, to Havergey, to give humanity a chance to do better next time.

So I remembered the wind turbines, and it seemed, looking back, that they represented everything about my society that was suspect. A good idea – in certain circumstances and sites, and *in scale* – hijacked and made into a catch-all solution by the greedy, the politically desperate, and every variety of hard-line ideologue who, while he knew nothing about the science, and probably hadn't even bothered to do any research (other than read the literature pumped out by the industry) would happily turn up with his chums to attack anybody protesting the damage that the wind turbines were doing to the land and birdlife. Or rather, the wind *farms*, as the developers called them (it was a commonplace that, the uglier and more inappropriate to location a development was, the more likely it would get a pretty name. Willowbrook Wind Farm. The Woodlands Executive Homes. Lakewood Retail Park. No sign of willows, or woods, or a lake, anywhere, of course. Just money, growing.)

I can't imagine the people of Havergey exhibiting any enthusiasm for the turbine when it was first discussed. But then, nobody could object. Even if Havergey had not been the property of a petty tyrant who did whatever he liked, whenever he liked, it should be remembered that, back when such things mattered, the island was under the jurisdiction of a country known as Scotland, a formerly proud nation, now so politically compromised that, not so very long before The Collapse, a foreign billionaire could arrive out of the blue and not only demand the right to build a luxury golf course over one of the most beautiful areas in the country, obliterating people's houses and gardens and at least one site of special scientific interest, but also, to cap it off, successfully persuade the government of the day to throw its full legal weight behind him, as his lawyers forced people out of their homes and off their land, pretty much on a whim. (That same billionaire would later become President of the United States, and one of his policy promises was that he would build a huge wall between the US and Mexico – for which, he insisted, a sheepish and utterly docile Mexican government would pay. Was this plan inspired by his experiences in Scotland?)

As far as that last Scottish government was concerned, any landowner could erect any number of wind turbines pretty much anywhere, no matter how absurd the location. When the people of Shetland – the real people that is, not the 'business community' – protested the erection of over a hundred turbines on an area of undisturbed peatland, in contravention of European regulations protecting rare birds, a respected Scottish judge upheld that objection and overturned the planning permission that had previously been jostled through the local council. The legal case was clear, on several counts, but the plan was also a crying out loud farce from an environmental perspective, because digging up that much undisturbed peat would release huge quantities of greenhouse gases (this is Environmentalism 101, in fact, on the same level as 'cutting down forests = bad'), thus adding significantly to the very problem that the turbines were supposed to be addressing. Meanwhile, covering the land with massive plugs of alkaline concrete (to stabilise the towers, which could be anywhere between 150 and 300 feet in height) inevitably altered the chemistry and structure of the soil for decades (well, to be truthful, nobody really knew how long).

This did not deter the Scottish government, however. They simply overturned the esteemed judge's ruling in a higher court, and went on their merry way. Interestingly, the company running the project was named, apparently without a hint of irony: 'Viking'. (Shetland was colonised by the Vikings in the ninth century and, though there is much debate about what happened to the original Pictish inhabitants, it seems odd that their culture and even their place names appear to have vanished overnight, unless we accept Alfred P. Smyth's contention that, 'all the evidence suggests that the Scottish Isles bore the full brunt of the fury of these invaders who were instantly conspicuous to Scots, English and Irish alike, for their brutality.') Nevertheless, even when the polluter company obligingly advertised its true nature by taking on the appellation of a brutal, murderous band of pirates, the Scottish government was still more inclined to support it through the courts than to uphold the will of the local people or the clear environmental imperatives.

So when Hugh Follansbee decided he wanted to cash in on lavish government subsidies and erect his wind turbine, nobody could have stopped him. It didn't matter that the turbine (the first of a planned series) was to be built, like so many others, on virgin peatland, at the wildest end of Havergey, a birdwatcher's paradise, not to mention a close-to-unique habitat for some very rare plant life. By that time, even some in government were starting to realise what a bad idea wind turbines actually were and, though nobody apologised for the huge damage done in only a decade or so during the 1990s and 2000s, some senior people started making the process more difficult to shove through. Still, it was a shameful period in those last years of recorded history. The one good thing that might have come out of it all was that those who really cared about the environment – the deep ecologists, the Earth First! folks, the true pagans who had found a wildness in themselves to match the wildness around them – knew they had to be cautious about their supposed allies in various Green organisations, especially political parties. The way the wind energy system was set up financially had been a huge confidence trick from the start: good for the electricity companies because wind, being so very intermittent, has always to be backed up by 'conventional' power plants; good for landowners, who raked in barrowloads of money for doing nothing, and good for politicians, who could say they were 'doing something' about climate change. Of course, they didn't advocate any serious energy saving measures – that wouldn't have helped with campaign contributions – and most people out there in la-la land were content, as long as they could keep their damned lights on.

It was all coming back to me. The disgust. The indignation. The sense of betrayal by people who should have seen through it all, but decided not to, because wind energy was renewable energy and 'renewable' – no matter how inefficient, unjust or environmentally costly it might really be – was an ideological matter. Which meant we didn't even have to think about the strategies we were adopting, we simply adopted whatever looked right, however cosmetic. We should also have stayed alert to the fact that, as soon as anybody comes up with a plan, no matter how sound, no matter how well-intentioned, no matter how urgent and necessary, a whole crew of parasites moves in and starts to carve out their share of the funding. We didn't take any serious measures to save energy, we didn't treat seriously any plans for smaller-scale, gradual or independent developments that might help balance energy generation, because everything had to stay on the grid (what would happen to the corporations' profits if people started switching things off, or going off-grid?). We went for big, cosmetic gestures that made us feel better about ourselves and seemed, for a time, to propitiate the gods. So by the time James Lovelock was comparing us to the Easter Islanders, it was already too late. Our civilisation had already failed. Now all that remained was for it to die.

In his autobiography, John the Gardener says something funny about history. He has been talking about The Catastrophe – dramatic changes in the weather, loss of species on a day-to-day basis, the oceans clogged with chemical waste – and he says out of the blue that history is always a battle between two kinds of people (if we exclude the wicked and the indifferent). There are those who say we must do something, now, to end slavery, or environmental destruction, or mass poverty, and there are those who say we have to begin by working out what needs to be done, and go about the task with total determination. He says the key thing is the finding out because, without understanding, action is worthless. But then, he reconsiders and adds: At the same time, we can plead that we do not understand everything yet, and so we are excused from acting. This is the huge difference between *wu wei* and passivity: there will never be enough confirmed factual information (if there is, that probably means it's too late to do anything) but we can shift from one mode of knowing to another, when the times demand it – and that was the great problem we seemed to have before The Collapse: we only accepted one kind of knowledge. That was our failure. We thought the only science was hard science. We were The Machine People. Guilty as charged.

★

I was going back over Chloë's document – I wasn't sure why, but I felt I had missed something – when Angharad came to find me the next day. I looked out of the window and saw that, over the meadow, the darkness has descended once more. I had completely lost track of time.

'What are you reading?' she asked, as I put the file aside.

'Chloë's excursion,' I said. 'I've read it once, but I thought… I don't know. I had the feeling I'd missed something.'

Angharad nodded. 'She was quite a girl,' she said. 'I wish I could have met her.'

'Yes,' I said. 'She seems quite… wonderful.' I thought again of her cruel digression on nobility. 'It was a surprise to find her lost for words, towards the end there.'

Angharad laughed. 'You're talking about the turbine?'

'Yes.'

'Yes,' she said. 'Follansbee's Folly. We've debated for years what we should do with that thing.'

'Where is it? I don't recall seeing – '

'Oh, we took it down years ago,' she said. 'Dug out the concrete. Prayed over the land, in hopes that it might heal. It will take a while, I suspect.'

'So where is it now?'

'We have it in storage. But we haven't forgotten it. In fact, it's part of a long-standing game we've been playing. It's called – Recycle This!'

'Ah.' I remembered how, even at the time, the blades were considered pretty well impossible to recycle – another reason to question the policy. 'I can't imagine you're having much luck with that.'

'None at all,' she said. 'So far, the only use we can find for them is in one of our regular ingenuity tests. As I say, we have those from time to time, just for fun. Public competitions, ingenuity tests. How to store energy. How to preserve food better for the winter months. Small things like that. And big things. So far, not much luck – and that's just one turbine. Imagine if The Machine People had lived on and been obliged to recycle hundreds of thousands of these things. And to think there were so many other options…'

'I've been thinking about that,' I said. 'And I've been wondering why it is that the wind farms stick out in my mind as one of our worst moments. We – Machine People.' Angharad smiled. 'After all, we did much worse things. We destroyed the forests, the prairies, the tundra. We poisoned the oceans. Why am I so much more offended by our follies than by our sins?'

Angharad shook her head, but there was nothing more to say on that subject. The Machine People were gone. Most of them, anyway. 'I've been talking to the others,' she said.

So, I thought. This is it – but I didn't say anything.

'We think you belong here,' she said. 'That's if – *you* think so.'

I nodded. 'I would be honoured,' I said.

'But do you think you're ready?'

'I don't know.'

She studied my face for a moment, in that disconcerting way she had. 'You have a choice, tonight,' she said. 'You can have dinner here, just you and me. Or you can go through the door to Havergey and join the feast.'

'The feast?'

'My kinsfolk have prepared a feast,' she said. 'In your honour.' She smiled. 'Though don't be too flattered by that.

We'll use any excuse for a feast.'

I laughed. 'Well, then,' I said. 'I can't very well let them down.' I thought for a moment. 'As long as…' I looked at her. She seemed solemn, all of a sudden. 'Do *you* think I'm ready?' I said.

She smiled, then shook her head again. 'It doesn't matter what I think,' she said.

WELCOME TO HAVERGEY

That day I saw the real Havergey for the first time – by which I mean, I saw the people, the community, that had come to live there. It seemed as if everyone had turned out to greet me as I passed through the door of the quarantine house and out into the snow, where the islanders were waiting, curious, no doubt, but what I most felt was the kindness – and, looking back to that first encounter, I can say that, if Havergey had done nothing else for me, it would still have expanded my vocabulary. Kindness. Grace. Honour. All words I knew, but hadn't understood till I came here. For me, and I imagine for most of those I had left behind, those words were like museum pieces, quaint, rather attractive, but outmoded. I could say a great deal about that day's kindness, and about the day in general, but for the moment all I will say is that, for the first time in my life, I felt I belonged to something. It had nothing to do with me. I had done nothing to deserve it. It was a gift and, again, I felt that I was understanding that concept for the first time – a *gift*, which has not only to be given, but also accepted. I think, if Angharad and Ben were concerned about anything, it was that I might not understand this.

Months have passed since then. I have continued to study The Archive – the originals, kept in the library, along with the coded notebooks that Max Jedermann left behind. Sometimes I work on them in the evening, after a day's work, and I am gratified to say that I have made some progress. I am not a cryptographer – but then, neither was Max. Still, for now, at least, neither of those facts seems an obstacle and I do think I will find a solution sooner rather than later.

Most of the time, though, I work in the gardens. Most people do, at some time or another. Every day we give thanks to the earth – it's not a religious thing, we just give thanks for thaw, for rain, for the first seedlings, for flowers, for our bees. I say it's not a religious thing, and it isn't, in any way I have ever understood the word, but then, as Ben says, if you start with the etymology and see where that takes you, any idea can be understood in a new way. The word religion, he tells me, comes from the Latin *religare*, to retie, to reconnect. To restore links that, for whatever reason, have been broken or lost. Seen in that light, it doesn't seem so absurd, or as offensive, as it once did.

Today, I am working in the orchard, pruning out apple blossoms. If we leave all the flowers to set fruit, we may only get hundreds of small, and not particularly sweet, apples; by pruning judiciously, we create a good harvest. It's a bright day, but gusty. Almost unconsciously, I taste, smell, listen to the air. Today it is salt-sweet, fresh, tinged with the scent of apple blossom. No trace of anything to come, but I taste it on my lips and I listen, because in my own way, I am also a Watcher. I feel, often, that I have been accepted into a kind of heaven – and maybe it's just the old human anxieties lingering on in my flesh, but I sometimes catch myself worrying that it will all end. I stand on the shore, at the edge of the sea (it seems so narrow, sometimes, this thin strip of water that divides us from the mainland) and I wonder when the next wave of disease or the first marauders might come. I don't know what that would mean, in the long term, but I know that everyone here, every last pacifist-anarchist-martial-arts-specialist, would fight to the death, if necessary, to protect this land. Not themselves, only, and certainly not such property as they – we – possess, but the land. The rivers, the woods, the garden, the meadows, the unseen elk in the forest, the sea around us. I wish my generation – the people I left behind a few months and forty years ago – had been capable of this same grace, this honour, this sense of community with the living world that, more and more, as I tend the soil, or bow down under the sea wind when it blows hardest through the rhododendrons, I have come to see as everything that is.

Little Toller **Monographs**

Our monograph series is dedicated to new writing attuned to the natural world and which celebrates the rich variety of the places we live in. We have asked a wide range of the very best writers and artists to choose a particular building, plant, animal, myth, person or landscape, and through this object of their fascination tell us wider stories about the British Isles.

The titles

HERBACEOUS *Paul Evans*
ON SILBURY HILL *Adam Thorpe*
THE ASH TREE *Oliver Rackham*
MERMAIDS *Sophia Kingshill*
BLACK APPLES OF GOWER *Iain Sinclair*
BEYOND THE FELL WALL *Richard Skelton*
HAVERGEY *John Burnside*
SNOW *Marcus Sedgwick*

In preparation

LANDFILL *Tim Dee*
LIMESTONE COUNTRY *Fiona Sampson*
THE FAN DANCE *Horatio Clare*
EAGLE COUNTRY *Seán Lysaght*

A postcard sent to Little Toller will ensure you are put on our mailing list and be amongst the first to discover our latest publications. You can also subscribe online at **littletoller.co.uk** where we publish new writing, short films and much more.

LITTLE TOLLER BOOKS
Lower Dairy, Toller Fratrum, Dorset DT2 0EL